SIT FOR A SPELL

MORGANA BEST

This is a work of fiction. Any resemblance to any person, living
or dead, is purely coincidental. The personal names have been
invented by the author, and any likeness to the name of any
person, living or dead, is purely coincidental.

This book may contain references to specific commercial
products, process or service by trade name, trademark,
manufacturer, or otherwise, specific brand-name products
and/or trade names of products, which are trademarks or
registered trademarks and/or trade names, and these are
property of their respective owners. Morgana Best or her
associates, have no association with any specific commercial
products, process, or service by trade name, trademark,
manufacturer, or otherwise, specific brand-name products and /
or trade names of products.

GLOSSARY

$\mathcal{M}$any Australian spellings and expressions are entirely different from US spellings and expressions.

Below are just a few examples. It would take an entire book to list all the differences.

For example, people often think "How are you going?" (instead of "How are you doing?") is an error, but it's normal and correct for Aussies!

The author has used Australian spelling in this series. Here are a few examples: *Mum* instead of the US spelling *Mom*, *neighbour* instead of the US spelling *neighbor*, *realise* instead of the US spelling *realize*. It is *Ms*, *Mr* and *Mrs* in Australia, not *Ms.*, *Mr.* and *Mrs.*; *defence* not *defense*; *judgement* not *judgment*; *cosy* and not *cozy*; *1930s* not *1930's*; *offence* not *offense*; *centre* not *center*; *towards* not *toward*; *jewellery* not *jewelry*; *favour* not *favor*; *mould* not *mold*; *two storey house* not *two story house*; *practise* (verb) not *practice* (verb); *odour* not *odor*; *smelt* not *smelled*; *travelling* not *traveling*; *liquorice* not *licorice*; *cheque* not *check*; *leant* not *leaned*; *have concussion* not *have a concussion*; *anti clockwise* not *counterclockwise*; *go to hospital* not *go to the hospital*; *sceptic* not *skeptic*; *aluminium* not *aluminum*; *learnt* not *learned*. We have *fancy dress* parties not *costume* parties. We don't say *gotten*. We say *car crash* (or *accident*) not *car wreck*. We say *a herb* not *an herb* as we pronounce the 'h.'

The above are just a few examples.

It's not just different words; Aussies sometimes use different expressions in sentence structure. We might *eat a curry* not *eat curry*. We might say *in the main street* not *on the main street*. Someone might be *going well* instead of *doing well*. We might say *without drawing breath* not *without drawing a breath*.

These are just some of the differences.

Please note that these are not mistakes or typos, but correct, normal Aussie spelling, terms, and syntax.

AUSTRALIAN SLANG AND TERMS

Benchtops - counter tops (kitchen)

Big Smoke - a city

Blighter - infuriating or good-for-nothing person

Blimey! - an expression of surprise

Bloke - a man (usually used in nice sense, "a good bloke")

Blue (noun) - an argument ("to have a blue")

Bluestone - copper sulphate (copper sulfate in US spelling)

Bluo - a blue laundry additive, an optical brightener

Boot (car) - trunk (car)

Bonnet (car) - hood (car)

Bore - a drilled water well

Budgie smugglers (variant: budgy smugglers) - named after the Aussie native bird, the budgerigar. A slang term for brief and tight-fitting men's swimwear

Bugger! - as an expression of surprise, not a swear word

Bugger - as in "the poor bugger" - refers to an unfortunate person (not a swear word)

Bunging it on - faking something, pretending

Bush telegraph - the grapevine, the way news spreads by word of mouth in the country

Car park - parking lot

Cark it - die

Chooks - chickens

Come good - turn out okay

Copper, cop - police officer

Coot - silly or annoying person

Cream bun - a sweet bread roll with copious amounts of cream, plus jam (= jelly in US) in the centre

Crook - 1. "Go crook (on someone)" - to berate them. 2. (someone is) crook - (someone is) ill. 3. Crook (noun) - a criminal

Demister (in car) - defroster

Drongo - an idiot

Dunny - an outhouse, a toilet, often ramshackle

Fair crack of the whip - a request to be fair, reasonable, just

Flannelette (fabric) - cotton, wool, or synthetic fabric, one side of which has a soft finish.

Flat out like a lizard drinking water - very busy

Galah - an idiot

Garbage - trash

G'day - Hello

Give a lift (to someone) - give a ride (to someone)

Goosebumps - goose pimples

Gumboots - rubber boots, wellingtons

Knickers - women's underwear

Laundry (referring to the room) - laundry room

Lamingtons - iconic Aussie cakes, square, sponge, chocolate-dipped, and coated with desiccated coconut. Some have a layer of cream and strawberry jam (= jelly in US) between the two halves.

Lift - elevator

Like a stunned mullet - very surprised

Mad as a cut snake - either insane or very angry

Mallee bull (as fit as, as mad as) - angry and/or fit, robust, super strong.

Miles - while Australians have kilometres these days, it is common to use expressions such as, "The road stretched for miles," "It was miles away."

Moleskins - woven heavy cotton fabric with suede-like finish, commonly used as working wear, or as town clothes

Mow (grass / lawn) - cut (grass / lawn)

Neenish tarts - Aussie tart. Pastry base. Filling is based on sweetened condensed milk mixture or mock cream. Some have layer of raspberry jam (jam = jelly in US). Topping is in two equal halves: icing (= frosting in US), usually chocolate on one side, and either lemon or pink or the other.

Pub - The pub at the south of a small town is often referred to as the 'bottom pub' and the pub at the north end of town, the 'top pub.' The size of a small town is often judged by the number of pubs - i.e. "It's a three pub town."

Red cattle dog - (variant: blue cattle dog usually known as a 'blue dog') - referring to the breed of Australian Cattle Dog. However, a 'red dog' is usually a red kelpie (another breed of dog)

Shoot through - leave

Shout (a drink) - to buy a drink for someone

Skull (a drink) - drink a whole drink without stopping

Stone the crows! - an expression of surprise

Takeaway (food) - Take Out (food)

Toilet - also refers to the room if it is separate from the bathroom

Torch - flashlight

Tuck in (to food) - to eat food hungrily

Ute / Utility - pickup truck

Vegemite - Australian food spread, thick, dark brown

Wardrobe - closet

Windscreen - windshield

Indigenous References

Bush tucker - food that occurs in the Australian bush

Koori - the original inhabitants/traditional custodians of the land of Australia in the part of NSW in which this book is set. *Murri* are the people just to the north. White European culture often uses the term, *Aboriginal people*.

CHAPTER 1

"Stop that!" I yelled at the house. "I'll never learn to bake if I can't practise." I pulled the cupcakes out of the oven and admired them. They were my best effort yet, only blackened on the bottom and up the sides. The sunken bit in the middle wasn't burned at all. I beamed.

The house made a grumbling sound.

"Turn the electricity back on now. Please," I added. I emptied the cupcakes onto a cooling rack. The cooling rack instantly broke.

The sprinkler system came on, drenching me and my cupcakes. "There was no fire this time!" I shouted. I didn't even know that the house had a sprinkler system. The house had been annoying lately. It had stopped watching Mixed Martial Arts and now only wanted me to watch baking shows.

No matter how much I tried, I was still having trouble coming to terms with the fact I had inherited a house with its own personality, a house which could change its rooms, turn on the TV, and terrify criminals by showing them the illusion that the walls were closing in on them. Still, that was no stranger than having to come to terms with the fact that I was a witch, a real live witch. When I found I had inherited the house and the cupcake store from my estranged Aunt Angelica, I had never imagined the strange things that were in store for me.

By the time I'd cleaned the kitchen, taken a shower, and was nicely dry, I had to tackle the problem of the cake. Camino, my elderly next-door neighbour and fellow witch, was having a Cluedo party that night and had asked everyone to bring a plate. The only trouble was that she expected something to be on the plate. And the way it was looking, my only hope was a No Bake Cake.

To my delight, the first recipe I found in my googling was a No Bake Fridge Cake. It looked simple enough, having only three ingredients. I simply had to soak chocolate chip cookies in sherry, cover them with whipped cream, line them up side by side on a plate, cover the entire thing with cream, and refrigerate for a couple hours.

What could go wrong?

I whipped the cream, remembering that Thyme, my best friend and also my employee at the cake store I had inherited from my aunt, had warned me not to whip cream too hard or it would turn to butter. I kept whipping. It hadn't turned yellow yet, so that was a good sign.

I had abundant packets of chocolate chip cookies, so I opened one and put it on the countertop next to the bowl that was ready for me to pour in the sherry. I was a wine drinker, but I was pretty sure I had seen sherry in the pantry. I couldn't find any, but there was a bottle of vodka left by Aunt Angelica. I'd never touched the stuff, but I figured it would make a good substitute. I read the label: '192-proof (96% alcohol).' I shrugged. That didn't mean anything to me. After all, I was a light wine drinker. It would have to do.

I soaked the chocolate chip cookies one by one in the vodka until they were about to dissolve, and then carefully moved them to the long, narrow plate where I coated them with whipped cream. I stood back to admire my handiwork. It had gone so well that I figured I should make two more cakes just like the first. After all, Camino had told me that the other witches—Thyme, Ruprecht and his granddaughter Mint—were coming, and also two of Camino's friends. I wanted to make a good impression.

CHAPTER 2

*R*uprecht met me at Camino's door and took the plates from me. "I have to go back for the third plate," I informed him.

He leant forward. "I'm not so sure this is a good idea."

"But they're No Bake Cakes," I protested.

Ruprecht shook his head. "No, I mean playing Clue," he whispered. "Cluedo actually, but Camino bought the game in the USA and insists on calling it Clue. All that aside, there have been two murders here lately and I've had my fill of solving murders."

I nodded. I had to admit that he had a point.

By the time I got back to the house with the third cake, everyone else had arrived. Camino made the introductions. I had not met her friends, Sue or Madison, before. Both ladies were somewhat younger than Camino. Everyone else I knew: Ruprecht, Mint, and Thyme. They were all seated at Camino's round cedar pedestal dining table.

Camino was clearly keen to start. "Let's start with cakes, and would anyone like a drink? Wine? Orange juice? Maybe a cup of tea?" She turned to me. "It looks like a nice cake that Amelia's made." Her voice held surprise and more than a hint of disbelief. "What sort of cake is it?"

"It's a No Bake Cake," I said.

"It looks lovely," Sue exclaimed. "I'd like some of that now, please."

I beamed. Camino set plates in front of everyone and I carefully distributed cake onto each plate. There were also cheese platters and a large plate of cookies, but everyone headed for my cake, much to my delight. No one had ever liked food I had made, and that is an understatement.

Between mouthfuls, Camino managed to speak. "Now that there are six of us here, we can play Clue."

Ruprecht raised an eyebrow and motioned around the room. "But there are seven of us."

"Oh," Camino said. "That's fine; I won't play. After all, I'm the host!"

Ruprecht shrugged in resignation and took a seat. The rest of us followed, Camino bringing the Clue board and game pieces.

I played as Colonel Mustard (like I always did). Sue chose Miss Scarlett; Mint picked Mrs White; Ruprecht was Mr Green; Madison chose Professor Plum, and Thyme decided on Mrs Peacock.

The game started smoothly enough. I had figured out where the murder took place, and was well on my way to finding out what the murder weapon was.

"Well, I think it was…" Mint paused. "Miss Scarlett in the dining room with the knife."

Ruprecht was the first to fold, explaining he couldn't refute it. I was next, and discreetly showed Mint my knife card. She jotted down some notes and giggled happily to herself. I would've thought it strange, but I was more concerned about how blurry she looked.

"What did you put in this cake?" Madison asked before taking another mouthful.

For some reason, I found it hard to concentrate. "I soaked the cookies in a bit of alcohol."

"Alcohol?" Ruprecht said. "What sort of alcohol?"

"I only left them soaking for a short time," I protested weakly. "And anyway, cooking removes alcohol from cakes."

Ruprecht was apparently doing his best to maintain a level stare. "But aren't these No Bake Cakes?"

"So?" I'd assumed that alcohol wouldn't have an alcoholic effect if it was soaked into food and eaten, which made sense to my drunken mind, but also must have somehow made sense to my earlier sober one.

I was greeted by a combination of gasps and laughter, but nobody stopped eating, so I assumed they were happy with it.

"That's a lovely bracelet, Sue," I said.

She held up her wrist in front of me. "I only got it this morning. It's from my sister, Barbara. Isn't it gorgeous!"

Everyone leant over to admire it. "Are those real sapphires?" Madison asked.

Sue shook her head. "I think the stones are turquoise. It's antique, Victorian actually. Camino, may I have a glass of water, please? My throat's so dry."

We continued the game in peace, and it was several minutes before I realised that I had my notes all wrong. At some point, I'd confused my clues and now had every single murder weapon crossed out, meaning that there couldn't be one, which was obviously wrong.

I sighed and placed my cards face down on the table. Everyone was laughing and having a huge amount of fun, far too much fun for a group of adults playing Clue. It was now becoming clear to me that I'd caused this by soaking those chocolate chip cookies in the vodka, as all of us were far more baked than any of my cakes.

Mrs White—that is, Mint—had found her way to the observatory, where she saw fit to accuse Miss Scarlett—Sue—of murder by stabbing. While this wasn't necessarily a nice thing to do, I felt as though Sue was overreacting when she clutched at her throat and then collapsed, falling face-first onto our Clue board, scattering cards and pieces in every direction. She then slowly slid from her chair to land face down on the floor.

In our drunken state, it was several long seconds before any of us had a reasonable reaction, with Camino being the first to run over and check on Sue. After several seconds of shaking her, we all realised that alcoholic cakes and our game of Clue were perhaps the least important matters to deal with.

I felt something other than cake stir in the pit of my stomach. Ruprecht pushed Camino aside and held his fingers to Sue's throat, checking her pulse. He paused, concentrating, before turning to us. His expression was grim. "She's dead," he announced.

We all sat in stunned silence for what felt like hours, although had probably been just a minute or two. I stood up and stumbled unsteadily over to Sue, grabbing her by the shoulder. Ruprecht looked at me and raised an inquisitive eyebrow, which I dismissed with a wave. He stood back and I pushed, rolling Sue over onto her back.

Her eyes were closed, which was a small mercy. Her mouth was open, and I leant in to smell her breath—nothing but alcohol. For a moment, I was afraid that my cakes had killed her, but remembered she'd eaten less than any of us. It could have been an allergic reaction, but that seemed unlikely. After all, she'd slumped over suddenly. She hadn't complained of pain or anything similar, apart from a dry throat, and there was no knife sticking out of her back. Perhaps...

The sound of Mint screaming cut me off. It hadn't occurred to me until now, but most of the people in this room weren't used to seeing dead bodies. I, on the other hand, had seen two in as many months. Madison grabbed Mint by the shoulders and ushered her out of the room.

Thyme was calling the police. "We should leave," Madison said, poking her head back around the door.

Ruprecht shook his head. "No, the police won't be long. They'll want to question all of us."

Madison's jaw fell open. "Why? It was natural causes, surely?"

Ruprecht replied to Madison, but I didn't hear what he said as he stared back at the body.

She was most certainly dead. I didn't need all my powers of deduction to tell that. I thought back to what had happened. We were playing Clue, and suddenly Sue had simply fallen. It was likely that was the moment when she had died, as she had not moved at any point afterwards.

It seemed like an internal problem of some kind, possibly a heart attack or a stroke. The question was whether it had been induced or had occurred all on its own. Other than perhaps having had a bit too much cosmetic work done, her body seemed to be natural. I was fairly sure my cakes hadn't killed her, as we had all eaten them. She hadn't eaten anything else while she was here, so poison seemed unlikely. Maybe this really was just a natural, albeit sad, occurrence.

At that point, the door swung open.

CHAPTER 3

*T*wo tall, muscular police officers marched in, taking in their surroundings. "Who are you?" one of them asked accusingly, staring directly at me and resting his hand on his gun.

"Oh," I stammered. "I'm Amelia, Amelia Spelled. I'm one of the guests." I recognised him as Constable Walker.

"Why are you here, with the deceased?" His tone was unfriendly and harsh. Before I had a chance to speak, he continued. "Oh, I remember you. This seems to be a pretty dangerous area around here," he said, concentrating his gaze on me, "what with two deaths in a short space of time on the very same street."

I was irritated. The man who had recently been murdered on my porch had nothing to do with me, as the officer well knew. His murderer was currently awaiting sentencing, and what's more, she had made a full confession.

Sergeant Tinsdell silenced him with a withering glare. "The ambulance is on the way," he said to Camino.

I was worried to see that the normally unflappable Camino was distraught. Her face was crumpled, and tears were rolling freely down her cheeks. Ruprecht had his arm around her, comforting her.

We were all gathered in the kitchen, having left the deceased in Camino's dining room. "I can't believe she's dead," Camino said between sobs.

"I need to start by asking her name," Sergeant Tinsdell said.

"Sue Beckett," Madison offered, as Constable Walker pulled out his notebook.

"Thank you. Now please tell me what happened, in your own words," the sergeant said.

"We were all playing Clue, and she just dropped dead." Camino burst into a fresh round of tears. Madison placed a cup of tea in front of her, but Camino waved it away.

"Clue?" Constable Walker said. "Is that like Cluedo?"

"Same game, just different names in different countries," Ruprecht said, "although there are variations between countries in some editions."

Walker nodded and continued taking notes. "Did Mrs Beckett have a history of illness?"

"No," Madison said. "As far as I know, she was as strong as an ox."

Camino interrupted him. "It is, um, was, *Miss* Beckett. Sue never married."

"And was she playing the victim?" Walker asked.

Ruprecht shook his head. "No one plays the victim in a game of Clue," he said. "And before you ask who the murderer was, I might remind you that it's a game of chance. The suspect, the weapon, and the room card are all in envelopes and are selected at random."

I was disturbed at where the conversation was going. Constable Walker seemed to think it was murder. At least that's the impression I was getting. To my relief, the sergeant did not appear to share his view. "There's nothing to suggest it's anything other than natural causes," he said, shooting a sideways look at the constable. "Our questions are simply routine. Nevertheless, as this is a sudden death of causes unknown, we have to report it to the coroner. This also means that a doctor cannot sign a death certificate. It will all be in the coroner's hands."

Camino looked up sharply.

"To be on the safe side," Sergeant Tinsdell continued, "we'll take samples of everything she ate and drank."

Thyme and I exchanged glances. A chill ran over me. Sue had eaten my cake, and plenty of it, although not as much as the rest of us. What if my No Bake Cake had killed her? After all, I had put my ex-boyfriend, Brad, in the hospital with food poisoning. I took a deep breath and tried to reason with myself. Brad had eaten chicken that I apparently had not cooked properly. There was surely nothing in my cake that could harm anyone. Still, Sue had eaten less of my cake than anyone else had. I felt sick to the pit of my stomach at the thought.

"What is this?"

I swung around and, to my horror, saw that Sergeant Tinsdell had opened the cupboard containing bottles of dried herbs, presumably the ones Camino used for spells. He read the labels aloud. "Mugwort, anise, white sage, five finger grass?" He turned to look at Camino. "Solomon's Seal? Do you cook exotic food?"

Camino was clearly at a loss for words. "Oh no, I, err, umm…" Her voice trailed away.

"Skin care," Mint said. "Camino makes her own skin care products."

The sergeant looked doubtful, but placed the bottles back. "Mrs Beckett didn't eat any of these?"

"Of course not," Camino said, rather too loudly.

The sergeant shrugged, and the two officers methodically worked their way through the kitchen, taking samples of all the food out on plates. They then went into the dining room, presumably to do the same thing.

"What if it was my cake?" I whispered to Thyme.

She patted my arm in reassurance. "Don't be silly. We'd all be sick. I ate a lot of it. It was probably a heart attack or something."

Sergeant Tinsdell came back in the room alone, notepad in hand. "I need to know the next of kin, and also the name of Mrs Beckett's doctor." He raised an eyebrow and looked at Camino. After she answered, he continued. "I will also need to have a description of the night's events."

We all spoke at once, and he held up his hand. "One at a time, please."

"Camino invited all of us to a game of Clue," Ruprecht said. "We all arrived at six, give or take a few minutes. Everyone brought a plate of food to share. We all ate and then started the game. It was just finishing when Mrs Beckett, err, died."

"Mr Foxtin-Flynn, if I could just speak with you in the other room." The sergeant nodded to the dining room door, and after patting Camino on the shoulder, Ruprecht followed him through.

"Why did he want to speak with Ruprecht alone?" I whispered to Thyme.

"He no doubt wants to know the details of how Sue died and he doesn't want to distress Camino."

I nodded. That made sense. "I'm sure the constable suspects murder. I can tell by the way he was talking."

Thyme shrugged. "Well, if it *was* murder, it wasn't one of us, so that leaves Madison."

She said it a little too loudly, and I looked up to see Madison staring right at us. She at once looked away, but I was sure she had overheard Thyme.

Was Sue murdered? She hadn't eaten anything

that the rest of us hadn't eaten, and she certainly hadn't been stabbed or shot. Poison was the only weapon I could think of. I suppose Madison would have had the opportunity to drop poison into Sue's wine. I shook my head. Surely it was natural causes. The sergeant certainly seemed to think it was. Still, I couldn't shake the nagging feeling that there was more to it.

Ruprecht returned and caught my eye. He, Thyme, and I hurried into the hallway. Mint and Madison were still comforting Camino, although Madison shot me what looked like a suspicious stare as I made my way past her.

"The sergeant showed me a photo from Sue's handbag," he said. "He asked me if I knew anything about it."

"Why would you? Thyme asked. "She wasn't your friend."

"I'm the least inebriated," Ruprecht said dryly. "He probably thought I was the one who'd make the most sense."

I hiccupped. "What was in the photo?"

"It was a simple photo of a house that I didn't recognise. I inspected it closely, but it seemed to just be a regular house. Though there were two figures in the window, it was impossible to make out any detail about them. Nothing about the scene made me think it was unique enough to warrant taking a photograph. I flipped it over and looked at the back. There was a small inscription that read '5/12.'"

"Is that a date?" Thyme asked. "It could mean either the twelfth of May, or the fifth of December."

Ruprecht shrugged. "He also said her phone was locked with a password."

"Why would the sergeant be so interested if he didn't suspect murder?" Thyme asked.

"That's exactly what I thought," Ruprecht said.

CHAPTER 4

J'd had a sleepless night, and it didn't help that my cats, Willow and Hawthorn, had decided to wake me up early to feed them. It's not as if they were underfed—quite the opposite, to tell the truth. They were even on special cat food for overweight cats.

I sighed and yawned widely. I didn't feel too good, what with the hangover and all. Thyme thrust a cup of coffee into my hands. "Drink this. You look like you need it."

I inhaled the wonderful scent of caffeine. There's nothing quite like the smell of coffee in the morning. "Thanks. I didn't sleep well last night, after, well, you know."

It was Thyme's turn to nod. "Ruprecht and

Mint have gone over to Camino's to see how she is. But enough of that! We have to get ready for the Customer Appreciation Night tonight."

I sighed again. The timing could not have been worse. Thyme had come up with the idea of a Customer Appreciation Night, hoping to draw in bigger orders from businesses such as conference rooms, and to attract other corporate orders. It was a great idea, and I had been looking forward to the night, but the death of Sue the night before had completely squashed my enthusiasm.

"The show must go on," Thyme said.

I nodded. She was right. We had invited our best customers as well as the corporate business people, but I had also invited the mysterious Alder Vervain. I was in no doubt that this would prove to be a problem.

My friends—Thyme, Mint, Ruprecht, and Camino—did not like the man, to put it mildly. The reason for this was that Alder's family, for generations, had been opposed to witches. In fact, Thyme had only recently told me that Alder was from a long line of witch hunters. And while the term was no longer relevant in this day and age, his own parents had complained to the local authorities about Ruprecht and Camino, and had even laid false accusations that they were drug dealers—anything they could do to make their lives miserable. And while Alder had shown no signs of following in his family's footsteps, my friends did not trust him at all.

I, on the other hand, quite liked Alder. He had recently moved back to Bayberry Creek and was a private detective. That was about all I knew, apart from the fact that he was awfully good looking. Alder Vervain was the one who had told me that I was a Dark Witch. I still hadn't had time to process the information, and I was unhappy, and even a little resentful, that my own friends still hadn't told me.

Alder had also told me that Aunt Angelica had been a Dark Witch too, and that it was hereditary. A Dark Witch was the most powerful of all witches.

Thyme tapped my arm. "You look a million miles away. We'd better hurry and get the store ready to open."

I nodded and took my coffee cup to the kitchen. I was half tempted to broach the subject with her now, but I had to prepare for customers, and then after that, the big night.

We had a run of bad customers all morning.

Sometimes it happens like that. There were the ones who slammed the money down on the counter when I had my hand out to take it, the ones with rude, loud children, and the ones who were angry that we only sold cakes and not coffee or a dozen other items.

I was about to shut the door—we always closed at midday on Saturdays—when Craig hurried in. My cheeks burned. I had developed a crush on Craig when I'd first arrived in town, but I soon found out his true colours. We had managed to avoid each other after that, which was especially hard for me, what with my baking usually setting things on fire and Craig being a fireman.

I looked around wildly for Thyme, but she was still in the back room. "Hello, Craig. What can I do for you?" I said in the most professional tone I could muster.

Craig did not look embarrassed in the slightest, much to my annoyance. "I'll have a dozen of the lemon blueberry cupcakes and a dozen of the chocolate peanut butter."

He didn't say 'please' and part of me wanted to say, "What's the magic word?" Instead, I carefully but quickly placed them in a box and told him the price with narrowed eyes. This time, I did not hold out my hand for the money.

Craig paid me, but instead of leaving, hesitated. I would never know what he was about to say—though, truth be told, I didn't much care— as Ruprecht and Mint came through the shop door. Craig left in a hurry.

"Camino is very upset," Ruprecht said without preamble.

I nodded. "I'm not surprised," I said. "I'm still in shock over it, and it would be so much worse for Camino, given that it happened in her house and to her good friend." I hurried over to flip the sign on the door to 'Closed.' When I turned back, Ruprecht was shaking his head.

"Camino says Sue was murdered."

"Murdered?" I echoed. "But who? How? And who would get murdered playing a game of Clue? Isn't that a bit cliché?"

Mint nodded. "It sure is! Still, Camino did a divination and she's sure that Sue was murdered."

Thyme looked up from wiping down the counter. "But who would murder her? And how did they do it? What was the murder weapon?"

I shoved a double cream cupcake in my mouth. Sugar always helps me think.

MORGANA BEST

Ruprecht crossed his arms. "Whether or not Sue was murdered remains to be seen. One thing we do know is that there will be a Customer Appreciation Night here in only a few hours. I suggest we turn our attention to that, and for once leave the murder, if that's indeed what it was, to the police."

CHAPTER 5

I was nervous about the Customer Appreciation Night. The idea had come to Thyme after she watched *The Real Housewives of New Jersey*—or was it Atlanta? I always got all those housewives mixed up. While the event was in part an actual appreciation for our current customers, the main purpose was to attract new customers. There were several conference facilities in the area, due to the proximity of the university in the next big town, so we were hoping that they would hire us to cater their cakes.

Victor Barnes owned the only conference centre in Bayberry Creek. I didn't know much about him. I had seen him once or twice, and word around town was that he was having an affair. I wondered how anyone in a small town could have an affair and keep it secret. Victor certainly hadn't been able to. He seemed polite enough, although not overly friendly. He always looked grim. Nevertheless, that was none of my concern. I simply wanted his business.

I was even more nervous when the time for the event drew close. No one had arrived. "What if no one comes?" I asked Thyme.

"Don't worry," Thyme said. "People always come for free food."

I didn't know if that comment made me feel better or worse, but sure enough, within minutes the first customers had arrived. There was no sign of Victor, one of our main targets for the night. Apparently one of the conference room managers from the next town had arrived, though, as Thyme made a beeline straight for a distinguished looking man and at once engaged him in animated conversation.

I picked up a tray with an assortment of cupcakes, and offered them to the attendees. I knew most of the people, although some were strangers. I was right by the front door when one of the town's three beauty therapists entered.

"Hi, Simone." My hand immediately went to

SIT FOR A SPELL

my eyebrows. "So sorry I haven't been back to have my eyebrows waxed and tinted. It's just that I've been so busy. I haven't gone anywhere else," I hurried to assure her.

Simone stared at my eyebrows and then smiled. "I can see that," she said with a smile. I was a little embarrassed in the presence of one so impeccably groomed, as beauty therapists invariably are.

"Do you make all these cakes?" Simone asked me.

I did my best to hold back my laughter. "Thyme does most of the baking," I said, and then looked at the dour-faced man walking up beside her. It was Victor Barnes.

"Have you met my husband?"

"Not really," I said. We shook hands. His grip was firm and I wondered if he worked out. I was about to launch into what I hoped was a good sales pitch, when Victor excused himself and hurried away. "I didn't know you were married to Victor," I said.

Simone selected a pastry from the table and smiled, but it did not reach her eyes. "Yes," she said simply. "We've been married for years."

"I was hoping Victor would consider us for the

cake catering at his conference centre," I said, pleased that I was so forthright.

Simone opened her mouth to speak, but just then Alder walked into the store. My heart thumped and I hoped my attraction to him wasn't written all over my face. Ruprecht, Mint, and Thyme all turned to stare at him. Simone did as well, which I thought somewhat strange. I had no idea they knew each other. Surely she didn't do Alder's eyebrows, too?

Alder weaved his way through the people and came straight to me. "Hello, Amelia and Simone," he said with a smile. "Amelia, why are you staring at my eyebrows?"

"Err, no reason," I said. "Do you two know each other?"

"Everyone knows each other in a small town," Alder said smoothly. He took me by the elbow and steered me into a quiet corner. Part of me was pleased, but part of me was a little dismayed that I had lost the opportunity to plug the business to Victor's wife. "Your friends don't look happy to see me."

I shrugged. "Well, it's because of your parents," I said.

Alder nodded. "I know. Still, I'm nothing like

my parents."

"I'm sure they'll realise that soon," I said, not believing a word of it. I was worried to see Thyme heading my way.

"Amelia, could I have a quick word with you in the kitchen?" she asked sharply.

"Sorry, Alder. I'll be right back." I followed Thyme into the kitchen.

She wasted no time coming to the point. "Did you invite him, or did he invite himself?"

"I invited him. I like him," I said truthfully. "Don't forget, he saved me from Dianne when she was trying to kill me."

Thyme shook her head. "He only called the cops. It's not as if he saved you in person."

"Well, calling the cops saved me, didn't it?" I realised my tone was defensive, even whiny, but I did trust Alder. Call it intuition.

Thyme rubbed her forehead. "Look, Amelia, I know you like him, but please be careful. His family…"

I cut her off. "I know all about his family, but not everyone takes after their family. Anyway, we'd better get back to the guests."

Thyme tapped my arm. "I'm sorry if I'm

coming across as controlling, but I really am worried about you."

I smiled. "I know you are, and I do appreciate it." I shrugged. I couldn't think of anything else to say, so I took a plate of gingerbread cupcakes out to the showroom. I couldn't resist eating one on the way. Thyme followed me out, and didn't say another word. I headed straight to Alder who was standing alone, although I did notice the eyes of several women fastened on him.

"How are you?" he asked with what I took to be genuine concern. "That must have been a shock."

"Yes, it was an awful shock," I said. "Poor Camino is distraught; that's why she didn't come tonight. Did you know Sue?"

Alder's expression fell. "Yes. I often subcontracted her to take photographs."

"She was a photographer?" I asked. I realised I didn't know much about her.

Alder nodded. "I regularly paid her to take photographs of simple cases."

My head was spinning. "I'm not sure I'm following you."

"I'm a private detective." Alder tapped himself on the chest. "I work on the insurance cases, but much of the work that comes to me is seeing if a husband is cheating on his wife, or a wife cheating on her husband. I always paid Sue to follow the alleged cheater and take photographs, while I was busy investigating more complicated, better-paying cases."

"Do you think that's why Sue was killed?"

All the colour drained from Alder's face. "Killed? But wasn't it a heart attack?"

I bit my lip. I could hardly tell him that Camino had done a divination. "The police weren't sure," I said. "They said it had to go to the coroner."

Alder leant closer to me. "It's always under the coroner's jurisdiction if it's a sudden death. That's no reason to suspect murder. Is there something you're not telling me?"

Just then I had a flash of intuition. I don't know how to describe it, but it was as if something had opened up in front of me. "*You're* not telling *me* something!" I exclaimed, rather too loudly it seemed, as several people turned to stare.

Alder did not deny it, but popped a custard caramel cupcake into his mouth. I saw that Victor was one of the people staring, and as he was

41

nearby, I took the opportunity to speak with him. "Do you like our cupcakes?"

Victor looked at me, and for a moment I wondered if he would reply. "Yes, they're very good."

"We do cater for conferences," I said. "Just with cakes, obviously, not meals. Some of the conference centres in the next town simply buy cakes from grocery stores, so we're currently letting people know that we can cater these high quality cakes for a reasonable price."

Victor's expression changed. "That would be useful. As you say, we usually send out someone to buy cakes, but they're the mass produced ones and not very good. I would be interested in talking with you."

I tried not to look as pleased as I was. "That's wonderful," I said in my best professional tone. "Would you like me to email you our conference packages, and then we could set up a meeting?"

Victor handed me his business card by way of answer. I thanked him and walked over to Thyme. "I overheard," she whispered. "Well done!"

CHAPTER 6

*A*lder grabbed my shoulder gently and pulled me aside again, much to the chagrin of Thyme. "Congratulations." He was beaming at me, but not with his eyes. He did seem to be sincere, though, but something was distracting him. "Amelia," he began, but his smile faded. "Why do you think she was murdered? Be straight with me."

"I'll be straight with you once you start being straight with me! What is it?" I realised that I'd asked perhaps a bit too forcefully, and Alder dropped his gaze.

"I can't tell you right now, but I…"

Before he could finish, Thyme grabbed me and spun me around.

"Let's go! There's plenty to celebrate." Thyme smiled happily and pulled me away and into the crowd. I looked back at Alder who smiled and waved casually. I knew we'd have to pick this conversation up later, and the thought didn't thrill me much. Sue had been murdered, but I couldn't just sit Alder down and explain how I knew that, especially with his history— no, his family's history. I had to keep reminding myself that his family's behaviour had nothing to do with him. Though, he definitely knew more than he was letting on, and it hurt that he didn't trust me enough to tell me. Truth be told, I figured that I was doing the same to him.

"Don't you think?" Thyme asked.

I'd been so lost in thought that I hadn't even realised she was talking to me. "About what?" I asked.

She sighed and rolled her eyes. "About a new line of cakes for Victor. We want to make a big impression, after all, and we haven't gone through all of your aunt's old recipes yet. I just went over all this! Weren't you listening?" She puffed out her cheeks angrily.

"Sorry, Thyme. I've just got a lot on my mind." I tried my best to smile, but only managed a weak kind of grimace, which was probably as unflattering as it was unbelievable.

"Cheer up!" Thyme was beaming again. "Everything's looking up. Just try your best to be happy for a night, and we'll work everything out tomorrow. Deal?"

Thyme was so sincere that I couldn't help but cheer up, if only a little. "All right, you win," I said with a sigh. "But we'll need a lot of grog."

Thyme smiled and poured me a glass of wine, which I quickly downed and passed back to her. She wisely refilled it and handed it straight back, knowing full well that when I said 'a lot of grog,' I meant it.

I assured Thyme that I was starting to have fun, and let her go socialise on her own. Besides, it was true—I was halfway through my second glass, and I was never one to handle my alcohol well. Still, I was a bit distracted by everything that was happening, and decided to talk to Simone.

I found her before long, wrapping up a conversation with a man I didn't recognise. I saw my opportunity and walked over to her. "Hi Simone!" I said, smiling sincerely.

"Hello, Amelia. This is going well!" She smiled back and gestured around the room.

"It is, thank you, but I was hoping you could help me make it a little better. Do you ever do wedding makeup?"

Simone raised an eyebrow. "I do, yes, but I didn't realise you were planning to get married. May I ask who the lucky man is?"

"Oh, no! No! It's not like that," I stammered. "I was wondering if you know any wedding planners. We'd like to start catering weddings, and I figured the best first step would be to contact some planners."

"Oh, of course." When she realised I wasn't getting married, a look of understanding washed over her, which probably would have offended me more if I wasn't already distracted and slightly inebriated. "I can pass along some emails to you tomorrow, if you'd like."

"That's great, thank you!" I hoped I didn't sound too forced, because I meant it. Having wedding planners as well as Victor making large orders from us could really benefit the business. "Do you..."

Before I could finish, from over Simone's shoulder, I saw Thyme approach frantically. "Excuse me, we'll chat later. Thanks again." I smiled and brushed past her, eager to see what had made Thyme so flustered.

"It's Kayleen." Thyme was clearly upset. I sighed deeply. You could always trust Kayleen to ruin a good thing. "What's she done this time?" I asked, not really sure if I wanted to know. "Eaten all the samplers?"

"Well, not yet, but she's getting there." Thyme replied, pointing towards the mean mail lady at the sampler table. I'd only asked as a sort of mean joke, but it turns out that Kayleen was well on her way to actually eating all the samplers. Like some kind of food-consuming machine, she was shovelling them into her mouth one after the other. I'd say she was eating like a pig, but I wouldn't want to insult porcine-kind. I decided that I had to put a stop to it before she made her way into the back room and ate our ingredients.

"Hello, Kayleen," I said, grimly. "I'm afraid these are just samplers, so everybody can have one and see which they like best."

"Yes, I know," she managed to reply between mouthfuls. "I have to eat a few before I'm sure. You make these samples much too small."

If only you'd been made a bit smaller, I thought, but held back from saying anything.

"Hello, ladies." It was Craig. He appeared from behind Kayleen, a sample cake in each hand. "How's everything going?"

I finished the rest of my drink and immediately knew I needed a lot more. I'd been on my way to relaxation, but seeing Craig again had set me on edge. "Excuse me," I said bluntly, not bothering to smile. I headed back to refill, downed it nearly instantly and refilled again— much better.

As I turned back to look for Thyme, I found myself standing toe-to-toe with a tall, middle-aged man. He greeted me with a friendly smile. "Hello, I'm David, Kayleen's husband."

My mouth fell open. "Oh, uh, hello." I managed to sputter out a sentence. "I didn't realise Kayleen was married." He looked a bit hurt when I mentioned this fact. "Oh, but I don't know her very well," I hurried to add. It was true, I suppose, which made me feel a bit better. Of course, the reason I didn't know her very well was because I was trying very hard not to.

"Ah, well, of course. I think I know you, though. You're Amelia, yes?" David had difficulty maintaining eye contact as he asked, and didn't seem very confident in his speech, though he came across as friendly. I immediately felt bad for him, given that he was married to Kayleen.

"I am, yes. Thank you for coming. I believe I saw Kayleen over at the sample table earlier, if you're looking for her." I almost felt bad about directing him to her, but I felt much worse when I saw her hand a cake to Craig and gently squeeze his hand. David turned to look.

"Uh, but, that was a while ago!" I said urgently, pointing in the other direction. "She might have even left by now, for all I know." I couldn't care less if Kayleen got what was coming to her—in fact, I'd probably enjoy it more than is healthy—but David didn't seem like the sort of person who deserved to have his heart broken. Of course, if he really loved Kayleen, there was probably something wrong with his heart in the first place. I was conflicted, but had enough on my plate as it was, and didn't need to deal with relationship drama.

"Yes, she does occasionally leave without me, so you might be right." He managed a sad kind of smile. "Well, Amelia, best of luck with the rest of the night. I believe I'll try to find my wife."

She's hard to miss, I thought to myself, but responded with the kindest wave I could muster.

CHAPTER 7

I made my way through the driving rain to Ruprecht's store, *Glinda's*, which sold both antiques and books. It had a decidedly wizard-like atmosphere and looked more like Dumbledore's office than anything. Ancient leather-bound books lined the shelves, and the scent of sandalwood and more exotic incenses that I could not name wafted from one end of the store to the other.

It was Sunday morning and that mercifully meant no work. Ruprecht had summoned us to talk about Sue's death.

Mint met me at the door. I shook out my umbrella and placed it in the umbrella rack inside the door, and then jumped as a loud crack of thunder rattled and shook the floor. In the mountainous area of New England, Australia, violent thunderstorms are frequent in the spring and summer months of the year. In fact, I had woken up to a tree down over my front fence. I would have to figure out what to do about that later.

"Tea?" Ruprecht said as soon as he saw me. He held up a tall green teapot adorned with zigzags and pin stripes as well as stylised shapes of flowers. "It's a new one I'm trying, Melbourne Breakfast tea. It has notes of vanilla."

"Yes, please." I looked around the table. I was the last to arrive. Thyme was patting Camino on the shoulder. Camino's eyes were red and swollen, obvious even in the flickering candlelight.

"Are we going to do a spell?" I asked, looking at the candles in the centre of the table.

Ruprecht shook his head. "No, the power's out, thanks to the storm."

I nodded and sat down. I liked thunderstorms, with the electricity hanging on the air, bringing the promise of something to come. The same feeling of something looming filled the room now.

"She was murdered, I tell you!" Camino blurted out.

Thyme and I exchanged glances. I had no idea how to respond, and I guessed the others felt that way too, because Camino's outburst was followed by a long silence. Ruprecht made a show of pouring tea.

"I did a divination and it was a murder," Camino finally said.

We all nodded. "But how?" I said. "If Sue was murdered by anyone present that night, it would have to be Madison, because it wasn't one of us."

"What was she murdered with?" Thyme asked. "What was the murder weapon?"

"She wasn't stabbed or anything," I said. "What about poison?"

Camino was crying softly into a tissue. "I wasn't able to do a divination to see what killed Sue," she said, "because I already thought it must be poison, given that we know that she wasn't shot or stabbed, and so on. That would've clouded any divination I attempted to do."

I had learned that much about divination in my short time of being a witch, or rather, in my short time of knowing that I am a witch.

Ruprecht poured himself another cup of tea. "Logic dictates that it was poison."

"And given that Sue died at Camino's, the poison must have been given to her just before she went to Camino's that night," I said.

Mint shook her head. "Some poisons build up in the system. It's possible she was poisoned over a period of days, even weeks."

"Sue didn't have any enemies," Camino said softly.

Ruprecht leant over to pat her hand. "She clearly had *one*."

A single tear trickled down Camino's cheek.

"Should we make a list of suspects?" Mint asked.

Ruprecht shook his head. "No. Let's leave this to the police."

Camino appeared not to have heard him. "I've been up all night thinking of suspects, but I can't think of anyone who would have a motive. Sue was a wealthy woman and her sister, Barbara, will inherit everything, as far as I know, but would Sue's sister murder her? I think not."

Ruprecht opened his mouth, but Camino went on. "And who else would have a motive, apart from Madison?"

"Madison?" we all said at once.

"Madison had a motive?" I asked, shocked.

Camino waved her hand in dismissal. "Madison didn't do it," she said firmly. At that moment, the lights flickered and then came back on.

Thyme leant across the table. "But why did you say Madison had a motive?"

Two faint spots of colour appeared on Camino's cheeks. "I shouldn't have said anything, so this is confidential. I promised Sue I wouldn't tell anyone." She looked around the table before continuing. "Sue was having an affair with Bob."

The others gasped, but I was still in the dark. "Who is Bob?" I asked.

"Madison's husband," Camino informed me, while the other three all spoke at once.

Ruprecht held up a hand for silence. I ignored him and pushed on. "But I thought that Sue and Madison were friends."

Camino shrugged. "I didn't say Sue was a saint, and I have no idea if Madison knew about the affair. Sue wouldn't listen to me when I tried to scold her about it. She kept insisting she was in love with Bob. She was sure he was going to leave Madison for her."

"No doubt the affair hadn't been going on for long," Thyme said.

Mint looked puzzled. "Why do you say that?"

"Small country town," I said. "Everyone knows everyone else's business."

Ruprecht smiled. "You're a fast learner, Amelia, and what you say is indeed true."

Camino nodded. "Yes, that's right. It hadn't been going on long."

"All the more reason for Madison to be a suspect," I said. "You know, she could easily have slipped something into Sue's drink while we were playing Clue."

No one spoke, but I could tell by the looks on their faces that they all agreed with me—well, with the exception of Camino.

"I've been friends with Madison for years," she said. "She's not capable of murder. And mind you, it put me in a difficult spot, what with Sue telling me about her affair with Bob. If Madison found out that I knew, she'd be upset with me for not telling her."

I murmured my sympathy. I was beginning to see Sue in a whole new light.

"Nevertheless, that is up to the police to decide," Ruprecht said firmly. "No good will come of our involvement in the matter; mark my words."

Camino snorted. "Hmpf! I think we should give the police some help."

Ruprecht made to protest, but Camino forestalled him. "I mean a spell."

"A spell?" I echoed.

Camino nodded. "Yes. A spell to ensure that the cops will find out that it was murder and not natural causes. A spell to make sure that they actually find the murderer."

Ruprecht let out a long sigh of resignation. "All right." He stood up. "I'll go get what we need."

Camino also stood up. "I'll help you."

"Do you both think it was Madison?" Mint whispered to us as soon as they'd left the room.

I shrugged. "Not a clue. She surely has to be a suspect, though, given that Sue was having an affair with her husband, and given that she and Sue had been friends for years. Madison must have felt awfully betrayed."

"We don't even know if Madison knew that Sue and Bob were having an affair," Thyme pointed out.

Ruprecht's return to the room stopped any further speculation. He deposited a white skull

57

candle on the table. "Now," he started, turning to us, "I will inscribe 'Find the truth' on the candle and anoint it with Clarity Oil. Amelia, Clarity Oil is made with rosemary, thyme, sage, and parsley. Well, that's the way I make it, at least. Many use lemongrass as well."

I nodded. I was sure I would never remember all of this.

"We will burn Solomon's Seal root with Bay Laurel leaves to bring clarity, insight, and wisdom," he continued.

"There's always the black hen's eggs," Camino said.

Thyme gasped. "Surely you're not thinking…"

Ruprecht interrupted her. "No!" he exclaimed. "It would be too difficult to do. Besides, we are doing a spell purely and simply so the police will find the murderer."

I shook my head. "This is all going over my head like the joke about the ceiling. Can somebody please tell me what's going on?"

"Black hen's eggs," Camino said. "You put one in each hand of the murder victim, and then bury the victim with them. When the eggs break, the killer will unintentionally reveal himself or herself as the murderer."

I thought that through for a moment. "But how do you put the eggs there with no one knowing about it?"

Ruprecht folded his arms across his chest. "Precisely!"

CHAPTER 8

*E*arly the following morning, I went to Camino's to check on her before I went to work. She greeted me at the front door, and I did a double take. This time she was wearing an oversized emu onesie. The brown-grey ruffles around her hips made her look like something out of a horror movie, and the beak on her head was as large as it was terrifying. She did indeed look like a giant emu, and an unfriendly one at that.

Camino had only just shut the door behind me when there was another knock. She opened it, and I could see past her to two men in suits. The one in front gasped and clutched at his throat when he saw Camino/Giant Emu. I didn't blame him.

The other man stepped forward. "Mrs Abre?

I'm Detective Marsters and this is Detective Stewart. May we ask you some questions?"

Camino and I exchanged glances, but before I could speak, Marsters looked at me. "And you are?"

"Amelia Spelled. I live next door."

He nodded. "Ah, Ms Spelled. Yes, you were present. We need to speak with you, too. Detective Stewart will question you in the other room, and I will question Mrs Abre here."

And with that, Stewart ushered me into the hallway and then into the kitchen. I was surprised how quickly the spell had worked. The fact that detectives were here meant that the police had now discovered that Sue was murdered.

The detective wasted no time in coming to the point. He pulled a long, silver pen and a notepad from his pocket, and without even looking at me asked, "How long have you known Mrs Beckett?"

"I only met her that night," I said, feeling guilty, although I had no reason to feel that way.

The detective looked up at me then. "So you only met her that night?" he repeated.

"Yes," I said. "Only that night." I had a feeling he didn't believe me, so I added, "I only just moved to town recently and I only met Camino and the other people in the town then."

"I see," he said. "And how did she seem? Was she anxious, or worried? Did she appear to be well?"

I shrugged. I wasn't expecting her to die, so I wasn't really studying her. Aloud I said, "I wasn't really paying attention."

"Did she seem short of breath or complain of being ill?"

I tried to recall. "No, she didn't say she was ill, but she did appear to be short of breath. I do remember her gasping from time to time. I thought it was just part of playing the game. She did look quite pale, but I don't know if she always looked that way,"

"I see," he said yet again, scribbling furiously on his pad. "And did you all eat and drink what Mrs Beckett ate and drank?"

I nodded. "Yes, I'm sure she didn't eat or drink anything different. She did ask for a glass of water, though."

The detective once more looked up from his scribbling. "And you've never heard mention of the woman around town before?"

I shook my head. "No. I didn't even know of

her existence until that night that we played Clue."
I still had the uneasy impression that the detective
didn't believe me.

"Have you ever been to Mexico?"

"Mexico?" I parroted. Why would he ask such
a thing? What did Mexico have to do with
anything? Had Sue been to Mexico recently?

"Ms Spelled, please answer the question."

"Sorry. No, I've never been to Mexico. Why do
you ask?"

He ignored my question, but then proceeded to
ask me the same questions about three more times.
I found it extremely irritating, and I wondered if
innocent people had actually confessed to crimes
just because they were worn down by the
incessantly repeated questions.

It was with some relief when I saw Detective
Marsters finally poke his head around the door.
"Please come with me," he said. When I was back
in the living room with Camino, he said, "I regret
to inform you both that Sue Beckett's death was
not an accident."

"Murder?" Camino asked coolly. She gave no
sign that she already knew the fact. "Then she was
poisoned?"

Detective Marsters swung his head to face her. "Why would you say that?" he asked.

"Well, surely it's obvious," Camino said. "I don't know any other murder weapons besides guns, knives, or something else that looks obvious. Plus the fact that we didn't know she was murdered at the time and thought it was a stroke or a heart attack means it was poison. Is that right?"

Detective Marsters frowned. "I can neither confirm nor deny the matter," he said. "We might have to ask you more questions later. We'll be questioning everyone who was present that night. That's all for now. Thank you for your assistance, ladies."

The two detectives made a beeline for the front door. When they were safely out of earshot, Camino took me by my arm. "The spell worked quickly," she said, but her tone was grim. "They now know that Sue was murdered, and poisoned at that."

"Yes, but by whom?" I asked her. "I know you say Madison didn't do it, but she had the opportunity, and if you don't mind me saying say so, she also had the motive."

"But we would have seen Madison put

something into Sue's food or drink," Camino protested.

I shook my head. "No, not if she was clever about it. Some of us went to the bathroom, while some of us went to the kitchen, and mostly we were concentrating on the game. We weren't looking to see if someone slipped something into someone's food or drink."

Camino walked over to a hideous, bulky floral armchair and sank into it. It squeaked in protest. I shot a look at the cuckoo clock looming over her. It was already past opening time, but Thyme always opened the cake store on Monday mornings. *That clock would be a good murder weapon*, I thought, looking at the enormous, carved deer antlers jutting out from the top of the wooden monstrosity. *I wouldn't want to be sitting under it in an earthquake.*

Camino rubbed her temples with both hands. "I'm sure Madison didn't do it," she said wearily. "I just know she didn't. It must be someone else." She paused. "We have to figure out who it was. Anyway, we'd better call the others and tell them that the detectives are on their way to question them."

"Good idea. I'll call Thyme, if you'd like to call Ruprecht." I headed for the door. I'd left my phone at home and wanted to warn Thyme as soon as possible.

I was about to hop over the low hedge that ran between our houses, when I saw Alder's car out on the street. What was he doing here? The day was certainly taking a strange twist.

I hurried out to his car just as he was starting the engine. I tapped on his window and he jumped. I walked around to the driver's side and he lowered his window. "Were you looking for me?"

"Yes," he said. "I went to your house and knocked on your door."

"I was next door at Camino's," I said. "Oh, did anything happen when you knocked on my front door? Did you feel strange?" I normally wouldn't have said such a thing, but I was critically caffeine deficient. In fact, I had usually had my third cup by this time, so I expected a caffeine-deprivation headache was on its way.

Alder appeared to be puzzled. "What do you mean?"

I shook my head. "Never mind." I had forgotten that my house liked Alder. It had never shown the slightest inclination to do anything horrible to him, unlike what it had done to several of my other guests, both invited and uninvited. That is one of the reasons I felt I could trust Alder. The house had always showed good judgment in the past—well, as far as people went. Its judgment in television shows was a whole other thing.

"I just stopped by to see if you were okay. I was worried when I heard that it was murder."

"So you already know it was murder." I said it as a statement rather than a question.

"Yes, with being a private detective, I soon find out that sort of thing," he said. "And since it was murder and you were present when it happened, I just wanted to come by and ask you to be careful."

"I'm sure whoever it is isn't after me," I said. "I don't think the rest of us are in any danger."

Alder frowned. "I think you should increase your protection, anyway."

I wasn't sure what he meant. "My house has very good security."

Alder shook his head. "I mean your own spiritual protection." He winked at me and then drove off.

I stood on the street for a moment looking after him. What did he mean by spiritual protection? As his parents had been vehemently opposed to witchcraft, talking about spiritual matters was the last thing I expected from him. Sure, he always said he wasn't like his parents, but still, telling someone to increase their spiritual protection was an unusual thing to say.

On the other hand, Alder had been the one to tell me that I was a Dark Witch. Did Alder know more about witchcraft than he was letting on?

CHAPTER 9

J also wanted to tell Thyme that I was running late for the shop. The detectives had kept me much longer than I had realised. I hurried through my front door and nearly tripped over Hawthorn and Willow.

I rushed down to the kitchen and emptied food into their bowls and then called Thyme. She didn't answer, so I wondered if the detectives were already there—or perhaps she had a customer. I left a message, and then hurried to take a quick shower.

When I got out of the shower, my phone's screen showed that I had three missed calls, one from Thyme, one from Ruprecht, and one from Camino. Just as I reached for the phone to call

Thyme back, she called me. "Amelia, can we close the shop for the morning, please? Ruprecht wants us all to meet and talk about what the detectives said."

I set the phone to Loud so I could get dressed while speaking. "Sure. You can all come here if you like. We don't get many customers on Monday mornings, anyway."

I raced around the house trying to tidy up. Of course, Willow and Hawthorn thought the broom was some sort of toy and kept pouncing on it. When I swept dust into a pile, the cats slid along the floor and scattered it. I managed to round them up and put them in the hallway, hurriedly shutting the door.

I stacked the cushions to make them look nice, and then dusted here and there. When I tried to get out into the hallway, the door would not open. Right then, the TV came on. Jamie Oliver was on the screen.

"No," I said to the house. "I don't have time for this! The others will be here any minute."

The house turned up the volume by way of response.

I sighed, and tried the door again. It did not budge. I had no other option than to sit down and watch Jamie Oliver give instructions on how to make pesto.

"I can do that already," I said to the house. "It doesn't involve baking."

No reply.

Minutes later, there was a knock on the front door, and the living room door flung open.

"Thank goodness you're here!" I said to a surprised Thyme.

Thyme bent down to pat Willow. "What happened?"

"Nothing, but the house locked me in the room with the TV and made me watch Jamie Oliver."

Thyme burst out laughing. I simply glared at her. I looked past her down the path to see Ruprecht and Mint in my yard, not heading to my front door, but rather hurrying over in the direction of Camino's house.

I walked onto the porch to see Camino stuck in the hedge between our houses. She was still wearing the emu onesie, but mercifully the hood was off. Ruprecht and Mint managed to extract her from the hedge without too much trouble, and led her to my house.

"Are you all right, Camino?" I asked her.

Camino staggered in the door, clutching the

emu hoodie and muttering to herself. She shook her head. "No, not after the cops gave me the third degree. I bet they think that I did it."

"Surely not," Ruprecht said, and we all murmured our agreement.

"Well, come inside," I said. "I'll make us a nice cup of tea, and some breakfast." I was worried about Camino. Her face was white and she was not acting herself. Her next words only confirmed my concern.

"I couldn't eat a thing," she said. She followed Ruprecht into the living room. I continued down the hallway to the kitchen, but once again, a closed door faced me.

I looked behind me at Thyme. "The house is driving me nuts," I said. "I wish it would stop. It's afraid of my baking."

"Aren't we all?" Thyme said, quickly followed by, "Sorry, Amelia. Have you been baking lately?"

I shook my head. "No, I haven't. I did try the other day, but the house turned off the electricity; that's why I had to make those No Bake Cakes. Now it's forcing me to watch the cooking channel."

Thyme frowned. "Perhaps the house has a premonition."

"What do you mean?" I asked. "Do you think

the house has a premonition that I'm going to start a fire with my baking?"

Thyme chuckled. "Well, it wouldn't be the first time." She addressed the house. "Please let us into the kitchen. I promise I won't let Amelia bake anything. I promise *I'll* make breakfast." With that, the door opened in front of us. Thyme took me by the shoulders and turned me around. "Amelia, why don't you go and ask people what they'd like for breakfast? I'll make it, of course. See if you can convince Camino to eat something. She certainly looks like she's lost weight in the last couple of days."

I had to agree.

Soon we were all sitting around my dining table, tucking into a hearty breakfast of toast, grilled tomatoes, and eggs—and none of it was burned. That, of course, had everything to do with Thyme and nothing to do with me. Camino was nibbling on a bit of toast, much to my relief.

Ruprecht set down his coffee cup. "Now, what did the police tell everyone? That is to say, what do we know? Concrete facts only, please."

I paused with my fork half way to my mouth. "Well, not much really. They weren't very forthcoming with me. Did they tell anyone else anything much?" Everyone shook their heads. I pushed on. "They did ask me if I'd been to Mexico recently."

"They asked me, too," Camino said.

Thyme and Ruprecht both said the same thing, and Mint nodded in agreement.

I scratched my head. "What do you make of that?" I asked.

"Did they happen to tell you that Sue was poisoned?" Ruprecht asked.

We all shook our heads. "Where are you going with this, Ruprecht?" I asked him. I thought if he had a long white beard he would look exactly like Dumbledore—the first Dumbledore—in the movies.

"Well, although they didn't tell us that Sue was poisoned," Ruprecht said slowly, "it's obvious that she was. I can only assume that the poison can easily be procured in Mexico and not in Australia. Why else would they ask us if someone had been to Mexico recently?"

I tried to gather my thoughts into some sort of order. "What if they had information that she met someone, perhaps someone who threatened her, in Mexico?" I looked around at a sea of blank faces.

"I think Ruprecht is right," Camino said. "I

think the poison must only be able to be procured in Mexico. That makes the most sense."

I had to agree. Television detective shows always said that the simplest solution was usually the right one. "Then where do we go from here?" I asked Ruprecht.

"Amelia, go and get your laptop," he said. "We'll google to see what poisons are available more freely in Mexico."

"And crosscheck against poisons that don't work immediately. You know, ones that take a few hours to work," Thyme added.

Mint butted in. "Days or weeks, even."

I went to my bedroom to get my laptop. I was surprised that Ruprecht was now showing an interest in the case and no longer telling us to leave it to the police. I fervently hoped that the reason wasn't that he was worried that Camino might now be the cops' Number One Suspect.

Half an hour of googling later, we had not found a single thing to help. "Perhaps Amelia was right," Ruprecht said with a sigh. "Perhaps the connection with Mexico isn't poison after all."

I shrugged. "It was just a thought. I don't really have an opinion either way," I said. "Would anyone like more tea or coffee?"

When I returned with fresh tea and coffee, everyone looked grim. Even the cats were motionless. The scent of caffeine wafting in the air did nothing to perk us up, no pun intended. "I wonder why the cops didn't tell us what the poison was?" Thyme asked, but nobody answered. We all just stared into the dark pools of our cups.

"If we don't know what the poison was, then we have no idea how long it takes to work, and that means that we can't get a good lead on the suspects. Anyway, let's look at them again," Camino said. "Madison—mind you, I'm sure it's not her—and Sue's sister, Barbara, who inherits everything, and who else?"

"What about Madison's husband, Bob?" I said.

"Bob?" was the collective echo.

I pushed on. "What if Sue was, well, harassing him to leave Madison, and he thought that murdering her was the only way to get rid of her?"

Camino shook her head. "It's a bit extreme, surely?"

"We shall add Madison and Bob to the list, nonetheless," Ruprecht said firmly. "So who do we have now? Madison, Bob, and Barbara. Is that all?"

Camino dabbed at her eyes. I had no idea why

I said it then; whether it was to distract Camino or not, I will probably never know. It was as if I were standing at a distance, hearing the words tumble out of my mouth. "So, I hear that I'm a Dark Witch?"

CHAPTER 10

*E*veryone's jaws dropped. Thyme jumped
to her feet, knocking a little bit of egg
onto the floor. Willow and Hawthorn pranced over
to it to claim it, and then swatted at each other,
scratching Thyme's leg in the process. She yowled
and jumped away.

Ruprecht froze. "How did you find out?" he
asked.

Thyme gasped repeatedly. Mint shut her
mouth and her hands flew to her cheeks, but she
didn't say another word. Camino's mouth opened
and shut. She looked like a goldfish. It would have
been funny, but the only feelings I had at that time
were hurt and betrayal.

"Why didn't you tell me?" I asked them.

81

Ruprecht countered with yet another question. "Who told you?"

"Well, is it true?" My tone was defiant. Thyme reached down to pick up the remains of the egg on the floor, but I glared at her when she straightened up.

"I suppose I can't take this out to the garbage now?" she said hopefully.

I shook my head. "Why did you keep it from me?" I asked.

"Now, Amelia," Ruprecht began in a placating tone, "we weren't trying to deceive you. Not at all. You were so shocked when you found out that you were a witch, and you were horrified when you found out that your house could do, um, stuff..."

I interrupted him. "I thought I took it all pretty well." I realised I was pouting, but I didn't care.

Ruprecht shrugged. "It's my fault. I told the others not to tell you. We were going to tell you soon, but there was a lot going on, what with the two murders in town."

"Three murders," Camino said.

Ruprecht nodded. "Precisely. Anyway, who told you?"

"Alder Vervain," I said.

There was a collective gasp. Ruprecht was the

first to recover. "How did he know?" he said, more to himself than anything.

I remained silent.

"I knew he couldn't be trusted," Thyme said grimly.

"Look, he didn't do anything wrong," I said. "At least he told me. How do you think I felt when I found that out, with all of you keeping it from me?"

Ruprecht walked over to lay his hand on my arm. "I'm sorry, Amelia, but I judged it for the best. I didn't want you to have too much on your shoulders all at once. Can you blame me?"

I thought about it for a moment, "No, I suppose not," I said, and with that, all my feelings of resentment evaporated. "But are you keeping anything else from me?" I shot him a penetrating look.

Ruprecht met my gaze. "No, truly."

I nodded, relieved. "And what exactly is a Dark Witch? I'm not like a zombie or Maleficent or anything, am I?"

Mint chuckled. Thyme's face was still pale. Camino chewed her bottom lip. Ruprecht sighed and gestured to the table. "Sit down, Amelia, and I'll tell you everything you want to know."

I did as he said.

Ruprecht, too, sat down. "A Dark Witch is a witch born with strong powers. Now we have told you before that some people who practice witchcraft have no innate talent at all, whereas others have various talents. For example, some could be psychic or even clairvoyant mediums. I suppose you could say that most witches fall into this category. Yet it is focus that makes a good witch. Even someone who possesses no natural abilities but who is able to focus strongly will be able to manifest and change their reality. I'm sure we've told you this before, Amelia."

I nodded, wondering where Ruprecht was going with all this.

Ruprecht cleared his throat. "To give an example: say someone wants to do a spell to make a nasty neighbour leave town. If the witch has strong focus and concentrates hard on their spell, then their focus will bring about the desired results. The witch does not need special abilities such as being psychic or clairvoyant. Are you following me?"

"I think so," I said.

"On the other hand, Amelia," Ruprecht said, "a Dark Witch, even without focus, would be able to make that nasty neighbour leave town in a hurry, to continue with our example. And if the Dark Witch does focus her or his powers, then she or he will become a very powerful witch indeed. And I suppose Alder told you that the ability is hereditary?"

I nodded, and Thyme muttered something to herself. I didn't hear what it was, but I'm sure it was rude. She really did not like Alder.

Ruprecht was still speaking. "Yes, your aunt Angelica was a Dark Witch, and you are a Dark Witch."

"That doesn't mean I'm evil or something like that, does it?" I asked him.

"No, no, no," Ruprecht said, while the other three shook their heads vehemently. "It's just an old term, probably so named due to the Christian influence. You know how the Christians rewrote the old pagan texts and made the ancient goddesses like the Morrigan and Kali into death goddesses as if there was nothing more to them?"

I nodded. That much I knew. As an avid student of history, I had always been dismayed that we do not have the original texts of some cultures. "I do understand that, but what exactly does Dark Witch mean?"

"It's just a term given to a powerful, hereditary witch," Ruprecht said, rubbing his forehead. "It means that you were born with the ability to manifest and change outcomes without really trying. That's why it's important that you practice, and that's why you keeping setting fire to stuff."

"So it doesn't mean anything bad?"

Thyme chuckled. "I would think starting fires without trying to is bad!"

I shot her a withering look.

"To tell the truth, it's often easier to manifest something bad than something good," Ruprecht said. "That's just human nature."

Mint spoke up for the first time. "Do you think Alder told Amelia so she would be upset with us for not telling her?"

"Yes!" Thyme exclaimed.

I sighed. "I know none of you like him, but the house likes him," I pointed out.

"Something's going on," Mint said. "The egg on my altar cracked this morning."

Ruprecht nodded sagely, but I was even more confused. "What does that mean?" I asked them.

"We all have eggs on our altars," Ruprecht explained. "They act as a decoy. If someone tries to attack us by magical means, the egg will attract the negative energy directed at us, and it will crack. Has anyone else's egg cracked?"

"Mine were okay, I think," I said to Thyme. "Were any of those eggs cracked when you made breakfast?"

Everyone laughed. "No," Ruprecht said. "You have to focus on the egg and say words over it before placing it on your altar. It doesn't apply to eggs in the refrigerator."

"Oh." I felt silly. I could see that Thyme and Mint were clutching at their stomachs and doing their best not to laugh out loud. Even Camino's lips were twitching.

"Still," Ruprecht continued, "I said to Camino only the other day that I felt negative energy around. I suggest we all be on our guard. Perhaps there are other witches in town."

"But surely we'd know if there were," Mint said. "And why would they wish us harm?"

"Could it be Alder?" Thyme asked.

Ruprecht glanced at me before answering. "As Amelia said, the house likes him. Nevertheless, we shouldn't discount any possibility for the moment."

"Could this be connected with Sue's murder?" I wondered aloud. "Or is it something else entirely?"

MORGANA BEST

Everyone shrugged, and I was worried. Ruprecht had been so against us looking into Sue's murder, but now he had dropped those objections suddenly and without warning. Was it because he suspected that the police would blame Camino? And now it sounded as if there were possibly rival witches in town. This was all too much for me to process. I needed answers, and I knew one person who could give them to me.

CHAPTER 11

*A*nd so I left work a little early that day, leaving Thyme to run the store. She didn't ask me why, much to my relief.

I headed out to find Alder's office, having never been there before. It was down a side street and along an old, cobbled pathway. I parked behind the town's only grocery store and walked down the little lane. Over the entrance to his office was a bottle green awning trimmed with gold, and the windows either side were covered by shiny black metal bars moulded into an intricate gothic design.

Two big pots of colourful geraniums stood to one side of the door, which was heavy oak with a big brass handle. I hesitated. Should I knock, or simply go inside? I gingerly pushed the door, and it opened onto a long corridor. To the left was an iron garden bench with blue and white cushions, and to the right was a door. On it, a plaque declared, 'Alder Vervain: Private Detective' in a bold script.

Again, I hesitated. I could not hear voices inside, and I had no idea if he had a receptionist on the other side of the door. This time, I knocked.

"Come in," a voice called out.

I walked in, to see a small office and Alder sitting behind a large desk next to an oversized printer. He looked surprised to see me. "Amelia! Please come in." He gestured to a low, well-padded chair in front of his desk.

I sank into the chair, feeling like a little child sent to the principal's office.

Alder frowned deeply. "Is everything all right?"

I craned my neck. "Yes. Well, no. That is to say…" My voice trailed away. "I have several questions for you."

Alder nodded, but I sensed that he was uneasy.

"I told the others that I found out I was a Dark Witch."

Alder smiled wryly. "And I suppose they weren't happy that I was the one who told you?"

"That's right," I said honestly. "They told me

that a Dark Witch is one born with ability, rather than an evil person."

Alder nodded. "Correct."

I took a deep breath and pressed on. "And they hadn't told me before, because they thought I was having trouble processing everything. And I was. You know, finding out that I was a witch, and inheriting the shop and the house, and so on." I had no idea if Alder knew about my house, so I was being careful with what I told him. I had no idea how much he knew.

"Are they going to train you?" Alder asked me.

"Train me?" I parroted. "Err, well, I'm not sure. I think they are already training me."

Alder appeared to be displeased with my answer. He looked down at the table, and then tapped his pen on it. "Do you know how to ground yourself, Amelia? Do you meditate?"

"Yes and no," I said. "I know how to ground myself, and know I should meditate, but I don't usually have time."

"You should make time."

I fought the urge to say, 'Yes, Master Yoda.' Instead, I changed the subject. "Remember when you said you felt I needed spiritual protection?"

Alder narrowed his eyes. "Yes?" He said it as a question.

"Why?"

"Why what?"

"Well obviously," I said, trying to keep the irritation out of my voice, "I am asking you why you felt the need to warn me. Did you think someone was trying a spiritual attack on me? Or sending me negative energy, or whatever you call it?"

Alder stared at me for a while before answering. "Yes, I did."

That took me by surprise. I didn't think he would admit it. "Is it directed just at me?"

"You and your other witch friends," he said. "And the fact that you have asked me the question leads me to believe that your friends are aware of it, too."

I chose my words carefully. "So not necessarily only at me," I said. "Could it be your family?"

Alder shook his head. "I am the last of my family, and whoever is doing this is working magic against you and your friends. My family, remember, were opposed to witches."

I knew there was something else I had to ask him, but my mind went blank for a moment. "Oh yes," I said. "Do you know what poison killed Sue Beckett?"

Alder shook his head. "The police are being very cagey about it."

"They asked all of us if we'd been to Mexico."

Alder hurriedly wrote something in a book, and then looked up. "Mexico. That's interesting. They asked me that, as well."

"They questioned you, too? Oh that's right. Sue worked for you sometimes."

Alder nodded. "Most of my cases are insurance fraud or missing persons. I always paid Sue to take photos in those cases where one partner suspected the other of having an affair. I think I mentioned that to you at your Customer Appreciation Night. I know most people think that's all private detectives do, but my main work is insurance fraud."

"Do you think one of your recent cases got her killed?"

Alder's eyebrows shot up. "I sure hope not! Like I told the police, it's been ages since we caught anyone actually having an affair. It seems most people are suspicious of their partners without good reason. Sue followed several clients' partners diligently and found nothing to report."

"Thanks, Alder. I'm sorry to turn up unannounced like this."

Alder smiled. "Don't be." His voice dripped with charm. "I'm always happy to see you, Amelia. Please feel free to visit anytime."

I narrowed my eyes and studied him. Was he flirting with me? I'd never had much luck with men. I just couldn't figure them out. "Err, thanks," I muttered.

I stood up and walked the short distance to his door. I opened it and then looked back over my shoulder. He was still smiling at me. Something occurred to me out of the blue, and the words were out before I could stop them. "Alder, are you a witch?"

CHAPTER 12

*A*nd that is how I found myself in Alder's apartment a short time later, with him cooking me dinner. His apartment was behind his office, on the ground floor—the whole building was on one level, and was very private. The open-concept living room and kitchen afforded views of the high walled garden through bi-fold doors.

Through the glass I could see masses of camellia flowers and potted azaleas, and honeysuckle weaving its way along the brick walls. I imagined the outside area would smell wonderful. The inside smelled of white sage and eucalyptus.

I had been rather shocked when Alder had invited me to dinner. Okay, that's putting it mildly.

My heart fluttered and my knees wobbled every time I was around him, so I was having a hard enough time steadying myself as it was.

Right now I was perched on a trendy red bar stool at Alder's kitchen counter, watching while he made Thai green pumpkin curry. If only my friends could see me now. They'd be furious! Despite that thought, I smiled to myself.

"I thought it best to talk about this in private," Alder said as he poured some coconut milk into the wok on his gas stovetop. "I don't want everyone in town to know I'm a witch, and as my explanation will be lengthy, and as I'd finished work for the day, I thought we might as well eat while I explained." He winked at me, and my stomach did cartwheels.

I looked around the apartment once more. There were no overt signs of witchiness, although I'd bet that the herbs in the glass bottles lining the kitchen shelves were not all used for cooking. There was a solid black mortar and pestle, the outside of which was adorned with a pentagram. The kitchen was all stainless steel and exposed brick, quite the industrial chic look. What's more, it was spotless. I hadn't imagined Alder to be a clean freak. He looked too, well, Goth, for that. I silently chided myself for my presuppositions.

"I still can't believe you're a witch," I said.

Alder looked up at me once more. "Surely you must have had your suspicions," he said.

I nodded. "Well, I did think you were mysterious." Silently I added, *And awfully good looking at that.* Aloud I said, "I thought you were hiding something, but I didn't know what. Plus this whole world of witches is quite a new one to me. The funny thing is, I don't think my friends suspect you of being a witch."

Alder's lips twitched, but his eyes looked solemn. "My parents and their ancestors caused your friends and their ancestors a lot of grief. The last thing they'd suspect is that I'm a witch. I'm sure they think I'm opposed to witches."

I nodded. "Yep. Most likely."

"And, if you wouldn't mind," he continued, "I'd rather you not tell them." He paused and held up his hand. "Of course, I'm not asking you to keep it a secret from them, as such, but please don't go out of your way to tell them."

I nodded, conflicted. My loyalties were to my friends. I could see that Alder appreciated that fact, but keeping his witchiness from them would make me feel bad.

"Wine?"

His words snapped me out of my reverie. "Oh, what? Um, sorry. Yes, please."

"Red or white?" He held up two bottles.

I shrugged. "As long as it has alcohol." I caught myself. "Whatever you're having," I added sweetly.

Alder smirked. "White it is. Chardonnay?"

"That would be lovely. Thank you."

Alder poured me a glass of wine. I took a generous sip, but his next words nearly caused me to spit it out. Just as well I didn't. "I'm a Dark Witch, too."

I managed to swallow the mouthful of wine, but it went down the wrong way. I coughed before recovering. "A Dark Witch?" I said hoarsely. "But how? Isn't it hereditary?" My mind was spinning. How could Alder be a Dark Witch? His parents— his ancestors, even—had been vehemently opposed to witches. How was this possible?

"I'm not adopted, if that's what you're thinking," Alder said wearily. "Yes, my mother was a witch, and so were her ancestors."

"But why, why?" I spluttered. None of this made any sense.

Alder shrugged. "They denied their abilities. I mean, I know that's obvious, but I'd say the reason that they were so opposed to witches was because they knew they had that very ability. It went very much against their mindset, and that is the exact reason why they were so upset about it. Does that make sense?"

I rubbed my forehead. "I suppose so. It will make more sense after I've had some time to process it." *Like a year or two*, I added silently. "Did your parents recognise your abilities when you were a child?"

Alder nodded, and a dark look crossed his face. "I had quite a difficult childhood. What about you?"

I figured that was his way of deflecting the question, but I answered anyway. The last thing I wanted to do was cause him to answer difficult questions that he wasn't ready to answer. "Not so bad for me, given the fact that my parents weren't witch hunters. I assume that's why my parents hadn't spoken to Aunt Angelica in years."

Alder stirred the wok.

I kept speaking. "You know, my parents were the last people I'd imagine to be witches. Well, I now know that my father was the witch; my mother wasn't."

Alder poured the contents of the wok into two dishes. "And you never met your Aunt Angelica?"

I shrugged. "I don't remember my parents ever mentioning her, but I accidentally drove past her house when I first arrived in town. It seemed familiar to me. When I found out that it was her house, I figured that I'd been there as a young child."

Alder handed me a plate. "Shall we eat outside?"

I nodded, and followed him to a seating area under a beautiful lime-green tree. "What a magnificent tree!" I exclaimed.

"It's an Alder tree," he said. "When I changed my name, I decided to name myself after it. It's deciduous, and only grows in wet areas. I suppose there must be an underground stream here."

I nodded. "I heard that this street is built on the grounds of an old river."

"True." Alder gestured to a seat. "The Alder is a protective tree. Its leaves and its roots are used in several magical traditions, from old Celtic lore to hoodoo. It was the tree of the Celtic god, Bran, and is the tree that marks March eighteenth to April fourteenth in the Celtic Tree calendar."

I nodded again and sipped my wine—slowly. I needed to have a clear head around Alder. The sun was low on the horizon, and the air had cooled to a pleasant temperature. Sunsets are always beautiful in this part of the country, and this one was no different, the sun's rays casting a beautiful pink and golden glow over the walled garden. The scent of jasmine and honeysuckle wafted along on the soft breeze. It was quite the perfect evening.

"And vervain," Alder continued, "is a protective herb. You probably know it as verbena."

"Verbena?" I echoed. "I have verbena flowers in my garden." I made a mental note to cut some and dry them.

"Vervain is used for general protection and to break a jinx. In fact, it was used in traditional European witchcraft for protection."

"I see," I said. "So you have chosen to name yourself after two protective plants."

Alder finished his mouthful, and then said, "Exactly."

I shifted uncomfortably on the garden seat. Sure, the setting was beautiful, under the Alder tree and with colourful plants in the garden, but I had never been in the presence of such a man. Call me silly, but I was powerfully attracted to him.

"I hope you give some thought to increasing your protection," he said. "Someone is working magic against you. I don't know if it's more against you personally, or against you and your circle of friends in general." He looked at me from under his long dark eyelashes.

It occurred to me that women would kill for eyelashes like that. "Do you have any idea who it could be?"

Alder shook his head. "Unfortunately, I don't."

Before I had a chance to respond, my phone rang. I pulled it from my pocket, intending to dismiss the call, but it was Ruprecht. I knew at once that something was wrong. "Sorry. I have to take this."

"Amelia, the police have just had Camino in for questioning. It doesn't look good. Can you come over to Glinda's?"

"I'll be right there," I said.

Alder frowned. "Trouble?"

I sighed. "That was Ruprecht. I have to go to Glinda's now. He said the police have been questioning Camino. I could tell by his tone that it's not good. It sounds as if the police suspect her."

"Surely not!" Alder was visibly concerned. "I'm sorry our evening had to end this way."

"I'm sorry too," I said sincerely. *Just my luck*, I thought. *Finally I'm having dinner with a guy who is not a psychopath or a narcissist, and I have to leave in a hurry.* I knew it was selfish of me to think that, but it was the truth. Sure I was worried about Camino, but I was also worried about myself.

CHAPTER 13

It was still a beautiful evening when I reached Glinda's only a few minutes later. I reached out my hand to knock on the door, but it opened in front of me. At first I thought it was magic, but then I saw Thyme standing there. Her face was white and drawn. I immediately felt guilty for being sad that I had left Alder.

"What's happened?" I asked her. "How bad is it?"

Thyme pursed her lips. "Pretty bad, I think. Anyway, I just got here, so I haven't heard all the details yet."

I followed her into the back room of the store. Ruprecht and Mint were there, as was Camino. "They think I did it," she said.

"Come on now, Camino," Ruprecht said. "Don't you think you're overreacting? Did they actually say they might charge you with murder?"

"Not as such," Camino said, wringing her hands. She jumped to her feet and commenced pacing up and down the room.

"Then what makes you think they suspect you?" Thyme asked.

"It was all their questions," Camino wailed. "They made me tell them every single thing I had done that day. They must have asked me eight or ten times. I went over everything I did that day, again and again, and then some. It's a wonder that I didn't have to tell them how many times I went to the bathroom and when. They also wanted to know exactly what Sue did from the moment she arrived. They asked if she was short of breath or had a dry mouth, and a whole bunch of other questions."

"But surely that means that they don't suspect you," I said. "If they suspected you, then they wouldn't have asked you what Sue was doing."

Ruprecht poured tea into a cup in front of Camino. "Drink this. It's chamomile and lavender with a touch of valerian. It will soothe your nerves."

"I think we all need some to soothe our nerves," Mint said.

Ruprecht raised his eyebrows and poured us each a cup of tea. The heavenly scent of the lavender was soothing, but my mind kept wandering back to Alder. "This is what I took from what Camino has told me of the police questioning," Ruprecht said. "I deduce that Sue was indeed poisoned, and that it must have been a poison that took a few hours to work. That is why the police wanted to know Sue's movements on the day of her murder."

"But that does mean that the police suspect me." Camino dabbed at her eyes with a tissue.

I made to protest again, but one look at Ruprecht's face silenced me.

"Ruprecht, do you still think we should leave it to the police?" Thyme asked him.

All our faces turned to Ruprecht, and he rubbed his chin. It seemed to me he was choosing his words carefully. "Alas," he said, "I must admit to doing a divination, and I do think that the police are looking in the wrong direction." He held up his hands. "I also have the impression that the answer is staring the police right in their faces, but they do not see it."

"If only the answer was staring *us* right in the face," Camino said dryly. I was glad to see she was no longer crying, and that a little colour had returned to her cheeks.

"As much as I regret saying this," Ruprecht said, "I do feel we might have to look into doing some of our own investigations."

I placed my teacup down on the table. "Well," I said, "if it was a poison that takes anywhere from a few hours to a day to work, then that surely narrows it down. At least we know she wasn't poisoned over a long period of time, such as with arsenic or thallium."

Everyone nodded. "True," Ruprecht said. "Amelia has a good point. Now, let us remember. What was the interval of time between when Sue arrived at Camino's and when she died?"

"It couldn't have been more than two hours," Thyme said.

Camino nodded. "That's right. So she was poisoned sometime that day. What if the murderer knew she was coming to my house that night to play Clue, and decided to frame me, to make it look as if I had poisoned her?" Her voice rose an octave.

"Now, now, Camino, don't go jumping to conclusions," Ruprecht said. "It might well be the case that someone did know she was going to your house that night, but simply wanted her to be in a public place when she died, to throw suspicion on many people."

I myself thought that what Ruprecht had just said didn't really make sense. I figured he was only saying that to placate Camino. "What poisons do we know that take a few hours to work?" I asked. "Surely there can't be many. Surely most poisons work immediately."

Ruprecht agreed. "Let's go to my office," he said, "and we will see what poisons do in fact to take a while to work."

We followed Ruprecht into his office and crowded around his desktop computer. "There's one that takes a few hours to work," he said, stabbing his finger at the screen. "Methylated spirits."

"But that says methanol," Thyme protested.

"Same thing, different names in different countries," Ruprecht said. "It's also known as denatured alcohol."

I leant over and peered at the screen. "It says

that someone can drink it and not have any symptoms for twelve to twenty-four hours. The symptoms include headache, nausea, abdominal pain, dizziness, blindness, vomiting, fatigue, and back pain. It says that by the time the symptoms appear, that it's too late to save them."

"Well, did Sue have any of those symptoms?" Thyme asked. "She did clear her throat a lot, and she said her throat was dry. I remember her asking for a glass of water, but she didn't say she had a headache or any pain."

I had to agree. "Let's keep looking,"

Camino stabbed at the screen with her finger. "Look at this," she said excitedly. "It says that cyanide can take a few hours to work if the victim had a full stomach. Perhaps that's why the police were asking what Sue did that day. If she had a big meal with someone, then that person could be the poisoner."

"Now let's not get ahead of ourselves here," Ruprecht said. "Let's look at the symptoms of cyanide poisoning." He typed, 'Symptoms cyanide poisoning.' We all peered at the signs and symptoms, which included headache, seizures, difficulty breathing, nausea, weakness, confusion, and cardiac arrest.

"Amelia," Ruprecht said, "can you make a list of any poisons that seem likely and we'll look at the list later? Put cyanide on the list. Now let's look for other poisons that take a while to work. Okay. It says here that the large dose of arsenic can take several hours to take effect, but don't put it on the list, Amelia. The symptoms are extreme and nothing like Sue's symptoms."

"Should we put it on the list anyway, just to be on the safe side?" Thyme asked.

Ruprecht nodded. "Okay, make a note next to that entry to check the symptoms."

"Look, here's one," Thyme said. "Ricin. It's made from castor oil. It says that as little as a pinch of it will kill an adult. Oh okay, it says it's made from the castor oil bean and is the part that's left behind after the oil has been extracted. Look at the last paragraph. It says that both Russia and the USA stockpiled it as a chemical weapon in the Cold War, and that the KGB and Saddam Hussein used it. Amelia, put that on your list."

"But what are the symptoms?" Mint asked.

"No idea," Ruprecht said, "but we can cross check it against symptoms later. The next one on our list is botulism. It says here that it's the most poisonous substance known to humankind. It says a single teaspoon would kill over one billion people. Lots of people have been killed by botulism —you know, food poisoning from contaminated food. It also says that there is a form of it from infected wounds, and that it's now available cosmetically in the form of Botox to treat wrinkles, excessive sweating, and migraines."

"I'd hardly call a migraine headache a cosmetic issue," Mint said.

"I'd certainly agree with that," I said, "but it doesn't say what the symptoms are, either."

Ruprecht shook his head. "I think we'll need to search symptoms, and the time it takes the various poisons to kill, separately. I can't see here where it says how long botulism takes to be fatal, either. This is not going to be as easy as we thought."

"It says here that strychnine can take two to three hours to work," Thyme said.

"No, it wasn't strychnine. Look at the symptoms," I said with a shudder. "Horrible convulsions and all. We wouldn't have overlooked those symptoms."

Ruprecht agreed. "It couldn't have been strychnine. How about colchicine? It says it's fatal within seven to thirty-six hours, and death is by paralysis of the respiratory system."

"I've never heard of it, but I'll add it to the list," I said.

"Aha, poison mushrooms," Ruprecht said. "Now we're getting somewhere! Right here, and it says no symptoms for twelve hours. The deadly mushrooms include Death Cap, Destroying Angel, and Fly Agaric." He turned to us. "Whatever the poison was, we now know something valuable. Sue had come into contact with the murderer that very day. We will have to find out exactly what she did that day and who she was with, and Camino, I don't want to upset you, but there remains the possibility that Madison was the poisoner. We're wasting our time looking for poisons that took a while to kill, if Madison slipped something into her drink or food that night. I know you don't want to hear that, but nevertheless it is an avenue that we must pursue."

Camino held up her hands in surrender. "I appreciate that, Ruprecht, and I understand you would want to look into it, but I'm telling you that Madison is not the murderer."

Ruprecht rubbed his hands together. "Let's get organised. We'll make a spreadsheet of all the possible poisons and then crosscheck them with Sue's symptoms and the time they take to work.

Then we'll make a list of suspects. We also need to know who Sue was with that day."

"But won't the police be doing these very same things?" I asked him. I was still surprised that Ruprecht had changed his mind about leaving it up to the police. Perhaps his divinations had revealed more to him than he was letting on.

"Speaking of suspects," Camino said, "Barbara, Sue's sister, will arrive in town tomorrow morning for the funeral. I've offered to let her stay at my place so I can keep an eye on her."

Ruprecht looked aghast. "Are you sure that's a good idea? After all, she is a suspect—at least to us, if not to the police."

Camino smiled, the first genuine smile I had seen on her face since that night. "Yes, and that's exactly why I want to keep an eye on her. I'll be in no danger, because if she did murder Sue, it was to get the inheritance. It's not as if she's a serial killer going on a killing spree, if she even was the murderer in the first place. I've met her before, over the years, when she came to visit Sue, but I don't know her very well. Nevertheless, having her under my nose will give me a good idea of what she's up to—if she's up to anything, that is."

Ruprecht shook his head. "All right, Camino. I can't tell you what to do and I would never presume to do so. But I don't have a good feeling about this."

CHAPTER 14

*E*arly the next morning, I staggered, pre-caffeine, out to the street to collect my two garbage cans. I dragged them down past my house into my backyard. I noticed that my gardenias looked a little droopy, so I filled the watering can and gave them a thorough watering. I returned to the house, ready to have a lovely cup of coffee after feeding Willow and Hawthorn. Both cats were already quite put out that I hadn't fed them before bringing in the garbage cans.

When I got back to the front door, I saw that it was open. Surely I hadn't left it open? I usually remembered to shut it behind me due to the persistent summer flies. I shrugged and walked inside. As soon as I set foot inside the house, I heard a noise from the living room and saw that the door was shut. I never shut that door, so with some trepidation, I crossed to it and opened it.

"Argh!" I screamed as I jumped back. There was a strange woman in my living room.

"Thank goodness you're here!" She said. "The door shut behind me and I couldn't open it."

"Who are you?" I said. The woman didn't look dangerous, and she wasn't carrying a weapon. Apart from that, the house had not attacked her, so I supposed she was harmless. I crossed the room to turn off the television. Once again, the house had the cooking channel on. I think the house had a thing for Jamie Oliver.

"I'm Barbara," she said. "Where's Camino? I thought she was expecting me."

"Camino?" I said. "Yes, she is expecting you, but I think you have the wrong house. Camino's house is next door."

The woman clutched at her throat. "I'm so sorry!" she exclaimed. "Camino said she was just popping down to the grocery store, and she'd leave the door unlocked for me if she wasn't home. I must have got the number wrong. Silly me. I'm so sorry. The door was unlocked, so I came straight in."

The woman's distress appeared to be genuine, and I had no reason not to believe her, apart from the fact she was a suspect. However, the one thing that did concern me was that Camino would leave a murder suspect alone in her own home.

"It's no problem at all," I lied. "I'll take you to Camino's now." *And stay with you until Camino comes home*, I added silently. I was not about to let a murder suspect snoop around Camino's house.

"Is something wrong with your television?" Barbara asked me. "The television got louder and louder. I tried to turn it down, but it didn't work. It kept getting louder and louder and then it kept flipping back to the cooking channel."

"It's just the wiring," I said. I wanted to glare at the house, but I had no idea in which direction to do so. "I've been meaning to get it fixed for ages."

"The wiring?" Barbara asked. "Does the house wiring affect the television?"

I shook my head. "No," I said. "I mean the television wiring. It's an old TV. I need to get a new one."

I took Barbara the long way—that is, not over the hedge—to Camino's house and knocked on the door. To my relief, Camino was home after all. I explained what had happened. I wiggled my eyebrows at Camino in an attempt to tell her to be careful.

"Is something wrong with your eyebrows?" Camino said. "Perhaps you shouldn't wear so much make-up, dear. You wouldn't want your eyebrows to fall off."

I narrowed my eyes. "I'm not wearing any make-up," I said through gritted teeth. Barbara had her back to me, and was bent over admiring a particularly grotesque antique. I caught Camino's eye and jerked my head in Barbara's direction a few times.

"Would you like some Advil?" Camino asked me. "With a sore neck like that, you obviously need some."

I threw my hands into the air and left.

Two cups of coffee and two happily fed cats later, and the world seemed good again. I still managed to get to the cake store early. Thyme was happily baking away. She was surprised when I told her that I had found Barbara in my house.

"But she showed no ill effects from being in your house?" Thyme asked me.

No," I said. "But don't forget, the house might have done that for a reason."

Thyme shrugged. "Anyway, Amelia, could you do the icing on those turtle cupcakes?"

"Sure," I said.

"You're getting to be a very good cake decorator," Thyme said. "You're certainly consistent."

"And I'm consistent when I bake cakes, too," I pointed out. "I consistently set them on fire. Consistency is not always a good thing."

Thyme chuckled. "Consistency is good for decorating cakes, however. And I've been thinking."

"Oh no!" I said in mock horror.

Thyme glared at me. "You haven't even heard what I'm going to say yet."

"I don't need to," I said. "Every time you think of something it ends in disaster."

"Name one time," she said. "Just one!"

I groaned. "Can anyone ever think of something when they're put on the spot?" I asked. "But just you wait. I'll think of all the times later and let you know."

"You do that," Thyme said, laughing. "Anyway, back to what I was going to say when I was so rudely interrupted by a certain person—I've been thinking about the murderer."

"Haven't we all?"

Thyme straightened up and removed her apron. "You know, we could make spreadsheets and lists, and compare poison times and types of poisons, and find out where Sue was all that day, or we could just get the murderer to reveal who he or she is."

I was perplexed. "How on earth are we going to do that?"

"Well, do you remember when we talked about putting a hen's egg in each of the victim's hands and burying the victim like that?" she asked.

"Yes, but…" My voice trailed away as the implication set in. "Thyme, surely you're not suggesting we do that?"

"Why not?" she said with a big smile. "I think it's a genius idea! All we have to do is put two eggs into Sue's hands and make sure she's buried with the eggs."

My mouth fell open. "You're joking, right? *All* we have to do?"

"It's a brilliant idea," Thyme said with a frown. "It's an old hoodoo working to reveal a murderer, a time-honoured way."

"But how on earth are we going to do that?" I

asked. "Do we tell the funeral director that they're the eggs from her favourite pet hen?"

"Oh, what a good idea!" Thyme gleefully rubbed her hands together. "Amelia, you have the best ideas."

"I was joking," I said in horror. "Surely you're not seriously suggesting we go to a viewing and put eggs in Sue's hands?"

Thyme looked somewhat offended. "Well, it's either that or waste time with spreadsheets and the like. Do you have a better idea?"

I chewed my lip thoughtfully. "If you want to do it, then you can do it," I said. "Just don't expect me to put the eggs into her hands."

A strange expression crossed Thyme's face. "Of course not." Her tone was less than convincing. "I'll do that if you can create a diversion."

I groaned. "No, get someone else to create a diversion. What kind of diversion were you thinking of anyway?"

Thyme smiled. I could tell she was enjoying this. "I don't know. Perhaps you could pretend to faint? Or choke? I'm sure you could think of something, and while you're doing that and everyone's looking at you, I'll sneak over to the coffin and put the eggs in her hands."

"I'm not going to create a diversion," I said firmly. Then I thought of one of those movies in which someone firmly says that they refuse to do something, and in the next scene they're doing it. I was determined that it wouldn't happen to me. "Anyway," I continued, "the funeral home staff will know that there are eggs in the coffin and they'll remove them."

"That's so true," Thyme said thoughtfully. "You're really very good at this, Amelia. Yes, it will have to be at the funeral, not a viewing. In fact, it will have to be just before she's buried. Do you know if she's going to be cremated?"

I shrugged. "No, I don't have a clue."

"That would be better," Thyme said, "because she'll disappear behind a curtain and I don't think anyone opens the coffin after that time. If you can create a diversion I could sneak in at that moment and put the eggs in the coffin. No one will ever know."

"Never know what?" a voice behind me said.

CHAPTER 15

My mouth fell open when I turned around. "Camino, what are you doing here?" I asked her. "I was worried that you'd leave Barbara alone in your house. She *is* a murder suspect, you know! I was trying to give you that hint this morning when I brought her to your house."

"Well why didn't you say so, dear?" Camino said.

I rolled my eyes. "Camino, please tell me that Barbara isn't alone in your house right now."

"No, she isn't," Camino said. "I had something urgent to tell you both, so I told Barbara I'd take her out for coffee. I've left her at that little coffee shop just down the road. You know, the one with the cranky waitresses."

"What is this important thing you have to tell us?" Thyme asked her.

Camino looked around and then stuck her head back into the showroom, presumably to make sure no one was there. "Well," she said in a conspiratorial tone, "Barbara told me something extremely interesting."

"What was it?" Thyme asked.

"She said that she had been here in town the day that Sue was killed." Camino's expression was one of extreme self-satisfaction.

"You're kidding," I said. "That's major!"

"It sure is!" Thyme said.

"And what's more, she didn't mean to tell me. I'm sure of it," Camino added. "We were talking and she just happened to mention it." Camino sneezed loudly and then hesitated.

"Bless you," I said. "Do go on."

"It was all over Sue's bracelet. Do you remember the bracelet Sue was wearing the night we were playing Clue?"

Thyme and I both nodded.

"I just happened to mention to Barbara that she wouldn't have been expecting to get the bracelet back in this sad way, and that Sue had very much liked the bracelet. Barbara let slip that she'd been driving through town, and as she'd already missed Sue's birthday, she had briefly dropped in at her house and given it to her."

I frowned. "Did Barbara say why she happened to be in Bayberry Creek that day?"

Camino nodded so hard that I thought she might give herself whiplash. "Yes. Barbara said that she always flies between Brisbane and Sydney, but she'd had a severe middle ear infection, so felt that flying was out of the question this time. That's why she decided to drive, and Bayberry Creek wasn't really out of her way at all."

"Do the police know?" Thyme asked her.

"I have no idea," Camino said with a shrug, "but I can't exactly go and tell them since Barbara's staying with me. Can one of you tell them?"

"Sure, "I said. "You go back to Barbara, Camino, and keep a close eye on her. Don't take any chances. Barbara has just gone to the top of my suspects list."

"Mine too," Thyme said grimly.

As soon as Camino was out the door, I turned to Thyme. "What do you make of that?"

"I don't like the sound of it at all. My mother always said there are really no coincidences, and it seems strange to me that Barbara just happened to pass through town on the very day that Sue was poisoned." She looked over my shoulder and said, "Customer! I'll go and call the cops about what Camino said," and sped to the kitchen.

I looked past her to see Kayleen. It was all I could do not to groan aloud. She waltzed over to the counter. "I'll have half a dozen of the double chocolate chip cheesecake cupcakes," she said, "for my man."

"Which man is that?" I said snarkily.

Kayleen stuck her tongue out at me. "You're just jealous. You don't even have one man, let alone two."

I shrugged. "You can't argue with logic," I said, as I boxed up the cupcakes.

Kayleen appeared to be on the edge of saying something rude, but she was forestalled by Simone's appearance. She at once switched personalities. "Hello, Simone," she said in a sugar-sweet tone. "I haven't forgotten my appointment."

"That was yesterday," Simone said.

I could tell that Simone was annoyed, but that fact appeared to be lost on Kayleen. "I thought it was tomorrow," Kayleen said with a dismissive wave of her hand.

"No, it was yesterday," Simone said again. "I texted you the night before to remind you."

Kayleen giggled. For once she was at a loss for words. She recovered herself after a moment. "Can I book in for tomorrow?"

Simone shook her head. "No, sorry, Kayleen," she said. "I'm fully booked tomorrow."

"Well, when can I book?" Kayleen said with a pout. "I really need some Botox. I know you ladies can't tell by looking at me, but I really am starting to get some wrinkles in my face."

It was all I could do to hold my tongue. I would have loved to point out that her face looked as if a heavy train had driven back and forth across it.

"I really do need Botox!" Kayleen repeated insistently.

"You're preaching to the choir," I said with a snicker. "You'll get no argument from me."

Simone crossed her arms over her chest. "I don't carry my appointment book with me, Kayleen," she said through gritted teeth. "That's five no-show appointments in a row. That causes me to lose income."

"Well, I'll just get my Botox elsewhere!"

Kayleen went to the door in a huff. Before she left the store, she pointed at me, her eyes narrowed.

Simone raised her eyebrows at me, and I shrugged. Yet something in the back of my mind was nagging at me. Botox—where had I heard that recently?

"Would you like some cupcakes, Simone?"

"I just came to give you the contact details of a wedding planner in Tamworth," she said. "I mentioned you to her and she said that she'd actually been thinking about doing cupcakes at weddings. She said to give her a call and set up a meeting."

"Thanks so much, Simone," I gushed. "That's very good of you."

"You're most welcome." She made to leave, but before she had even gone two paces, I spoke again.

"Simone, you do Botox?"

"Yes," she said. She looked surprised, but then again she always looked surprised, given that she had shaved off her eyebrows and pencilled them in half way to her hairline. "But you don't need Botox! You're too young. I do have clients your age, but I always try to talk them out of it. On the other hand, you could do with a boob job. I can give you a reference to a good plastic surgeon."

I was offended. What was wrong with my boobs? Sure, they weren't that big, but I thought they were fine. I tried to bring my attention back to the subject at hand. "Someone mentioned Botox to me the other day, and I can't for the life of me remember who it was," I said.

"Please refer them to me when you remember who it was," Simone said.

"I sure will."

"Thanks, Amelia. Wasn't it horrible what happened to poor Sue Beckett?" she said. "That poor woman came to me to get her regular Botox treatment the day that she died. She seemed so full of life then, and not sick at all. It just goes to show, doesn't it?"

I was perplexed. "It just goes to show what?" I asked her.

Simone's eyes grew wide. "It just goes to show that you never know when you'll drop dead," she said dramatically. Her eyebrows went even higher.

"Oh, yes," I said slowly. Simone left the shop after her cheerful pronouncement, and then it hit me. I remembered where the recent talk about Botox had been. Ruprecht had mentioned that botulism was one of the poisons that took a few hours to work. Yet surely if Simone had given Sue an overdose of Botox and killed her, why would she tell me that Sue had gone to her that day? And could cosmetic Botox even kill someone? I needed to find out. I needed to know whether to add Simone to my suspect list.

I went into the back room. "Hey, Amelia, could you please do the cream cheese icing on those raspberry peach blossom cupcakes?" Thyme said as soon as she saw me.

"I'll get right on it," I said. "What did the cops say?"

Thyme slapped herself on her forehead. "Oh, I completely forgot. I'll call them now."

"Well, there's something else you can tell them," I said. "Simone, the beauty therapist, was just in, and she told me that Sue was her client. She gave her Botox the day that she died."

Thyme's mouth fell open. "You're kidding!"

"You'd better tell the cops that as well," I said. "I mean, they could already know, but it's better to be safe than sorry. Anyway, can cosmetic Botox kill someone?"

"We'll have to find out," Thyme said, "but I'll call the cops right now and tell them both of those things."

CHAPTER 16

"**I**f I see Jamie Oliver one more time, I'll scream!" I said to the house. "I almost prefer Mixed Martial Arts." I jumped up to turn off the TV, but as soon as I did, it came right back on, and even louder this time.

I shook my finger at the house. "Please stop!" I said. "I'm trying to find out if Botox can kill someone, cosmetic Botox that is, and you're not helping."

As if by way of reply, the volume increased. I groaned and put my head in my hands. I crossed to the cedar chiffonier and opened the top drawer, from which I pulled out the set of earbuds that had come with my iPhone—and what a welcome sight they were. I sat back down, earplugs firmly in place, and recommenced my search.

It took me ages to wade through all the information. There were many forums, with people on one side angrily saying that Botox is perfectly harmless, while others alleged that they had suffered terrible side effects. But as far as I could tell, only one person had died from an injection of cosmetic botulinum. That meant death by accidental Botox injection was unlikely, so if Sue had been killed by Botox, it would have had to be deliberate.

I then searched to see if anyone had been murdered by Botox. I groaned. I only turned up a reference to an episode of *Sherlock*. I vaguely remembered seeing a movie ages ago where the victim had been killed by wound botulism, but I couldn't even remember the name of the movie. I simply remembered that the murderer had applied the botulism toxin to rose thorns, knowing that the victim-to-be was a keen gardener. Trying to remember was driving me nuts. I wanted to call Alder and ask him if he knew anything about it, but I knew the real reason I wanted to call him, and it had nothing to do with botulism.

I stood up and stretched, and pulled out my

earbuds. I felt at a loose end, and I was somewhat irritated. I got out a piece of paper and wrote 'Suspects' at the top. Under 'Suspects' I wrote: Madison, Bob, Barbara, Simone. Madison had a motive because Sue was having an affair with her husband, Bob. And Bob possibly had a motive, because he was having an affair with Sue. And then there was Barbara. She was to inherit all of Sue's fortune. I have no idea if Simone had a motive for murder, but she certainly had a suitable murder weapon. Was there anyone else? The police also suspected Camino.

Perhaps there was another heir apart from Barbara. We would not know until the reading of the will. I'd love to be a fly on the wall at that reading. Maybe there was a way we could hide a bug in the room and hear what was said.

At any rate, Thyme seemed quite certain that her hoodoo working would be effective. She kept going on and on about placing the eggs in Sue's hands at the funeral. We had found out that, after the police released her body, Sue would be cremated. Thyme said that this would mean that the murderer would be revealed sooner, because this spell went into action when the eggs were destroyed. I wish I shared her confidence.

I heard my phone, but I couldn't remember where I had put it. I looked around the living room, but there was no sign of it. Just as I walked into the hallway, it stopped. I sighed and turned to walk back to the living room, but I had only taken one step when the phone rang again. This time, I realised the sound was coming from my bedroom. A portent of doom hit me as soon as I saw the name. I slid my finger across the screen. "Ruprecht, what's happened?"

"It's Camino," he said. "She's been arrested."

"What?" I screeched. "You're kidding."

"I wish I were."

"How could they arrest Camino?" I said. "It doesn't make any sense."

"Well, there's something you don't know, Amelia," Ruprecht said. "The police found a syringe of botulinum in Camino's house."

"Botulinum?" I echoed. "But I've just been researching botulism." My head was spinning. "What do you mean; they found a syringe of botulism in Camino's house?"

"Obviously it was planted there," Ruprecht said. "That means the murderer has had access to Camino's house."

"Barbara!" I exclaimed. "Barbara is staying

with Camino! Barbara inherits everything from Sue. Is Camino still down at the police station?"

"No," Ruprecht said.

I let out a long sigh. "That's a relief."

"No, Amelia," Ruprecht said. "I regret to say that she's in the watch house."

"The watch house? What's that?" I asked him. I'd never heard of a watch house. It made me think of *F Troop*. Oh, I think that was called the watchtower. At any rate, it was my favourite television series when I was a child. My mind tends to wander when I'm stressed.

"The watch house is where they keep prisoners between the time they arrest them and the time the prisoner appears before a magistrate for the bail hearing," Ruprecht explained.

"Does that mean Camino will be in jail overnight?" I asked, horrified.

"Yes, but it would've been worse if it had been Friday night. Then she would have had to stay in the watch house until Monday morning."

"I don't really understand how this all works."

It was Ruprecht's turn to sigh. "Camino has been arrested and charged with homicide. There will be a hearing tomorrow morning to see whether she'll get bail," Ruprecht said.

"Does anyone charged with homicide ever get out on bail?"

There was a pause, and I imagined that Ruprecht was nodding. "I spoke with Camino's lawyer just before I called you," he finally said, "and he told me that the fairly new bail laws in New South Wales make it more likely. Camino doesn't have a criminal record; she is not a flight risk, and he said that the police don't really have a motive. And as you pointed out, Sue's sister, Barbara, who will inherit, was staying with Camino at the time and could easily have planted the syringe. He will argue that point in court tomorrow. He thinks there's a good chance Camino will be released on bail. He was surprised she was charged in the first place."

I could barely bring myself to say the words. "But what if she isn't granted bail? How long would she have to stay in jail, or the watch house, or whatever, until her trial?"

"It could be as long as two years," Ruprecht said, "but we won't let that happen. We will do everything in our power to have Camino released, and we will find the murderer by any means possible."

I bit my lip. I still couldn't believe that Camino

had been arrested. What possible motive could she have? She didn't stand to inherit anything, as far as I knew. Now that was a thought. "Ruprecht, it just occurred to me that perhaps Camino does inherit something in Sue's will. That would give her a motive, as far as the police are concerned."

"Yes, that thought had occurred to me, too," he said. "I asked the lawyer. He said it's highly unlikely the lawyer would divulge that information to the police. The will is going to be read after the funeral."

"Wait a minute," I said. "I thought you were speaking to Camino's lawyer. Does she have two lawyers?"

"I meant Sue's lawyer, not Camino's. At any rate, I secured a top criminal lawyer for Camino."

"Oh, silly me," I said. "Yes, of course. I'm just in such a state of panic about Camino."

"You and me both," Ruprecht said.

$\mathcal{I}$t was an anxious morning at the cake store. There weren't many customers, so the morning seemed to drag on. I occupied myself with making icing, while Thyme baked cakes. Ruprecht had said he would call us as soon as the bail hearing was over.

"I wish we could've gone to the courthouse," I said to Thyme.

"We can't afford the time away from the shop, Amelia, as you know," she said. "Plus, I would be far more anxious if we were there because we'd make Camino more anxious."

"Yes, I'm sure you're right." I slathered some cream cheese icing on the cupcake in front of me.

"Hey," Thyme said. "You look like you're trying to murder that cake."

I waved the spatula at her. "All this waiting around is driving me crazy!"

Just then the shop's phone rang. Thyme and I both sprinted for it, but Thyme reached it first. I could tell by the look on her face that it wasn't Ruprecht. "Yes, we are open until five," she said. "Goodbye."

"Bummer, I thought that was Ruprecht," I said sadly.

Right then Ruprecht and Camino walked through the door. I threw my arms around Camino. "I'm so glad to see you," I said. "Are you all right?"

"Not really," she said. "It was a horrible experience."

Thyme rushed over to embrace Camino. "Why didn't you call us, Ruprecht?"

Ruprecht shook his head. "Camino just wanted to get out of there as soon as possible." He nodded at Camino and raised his eyebrows.

I looked at Camino. I didn't expect she would be looking happy, but she was white and drawn, even worse than I had imagined she would look.

"That was the worst experience of my life," she

said in a small voice. "The watchhouse was a nightmare. It was cold, and I didn't even have a pillow or a blanket. There was no natural light. They didn't even give me any clothes. I had to sleep in these clothes, the same ones I'm wearing now. Can you believe it?" She swept her hand up and down her body.

"Did the prosecution oppose bail?" I asked.

"Yes," Ruprecht said, "but only half-heartedly. Camino's lawyer pointed out that she had no motive."

Camino covered her face with her hands. "I can't take any more. It's all too much. I can't believe anyone would think I'd ever murder anyone." She dissolved into tears.

Ruprecht handed her a white linen handkerchief with the initials 'RFF' embroidered on the hem. I had never seen a white linen handkerchief before, much less a fancy, embroidered one. I dragged my mind back to the situation at hand. Ruprecht was speaking. "Camino, I insist that you stay with me. I've taken the liberty of calling Barbara and suggesting she stays in a motel, given the circumstances."

Caminos hand flew to her mouth. "She doesn't think I killed her sister, does she?"

Ruprecht hurried to reassure her. "Oh no, of course not, Camino. You mustn't think such a thing! It's just that it's safer if you don't return to your home, given that the murderer has been inside your home and planted evidence."

"Do you think it was Barbara?" I blurted out unwisely. I was worried that my words might cause Camino distress.

To the contrary, Camino narrowed her eyes and spoke firmly. "Yes, that's exactly what I was thinking, and surely the police must be thinking it, too. I can't believe they arrested me when I don't stand to inherit anything, and Barbara's the one who will inherit all of Sue's estate."

Thyme took Camino by the arm. "Come into the back room," she said. "I'll make you a nice cup of hot tea."

"That would be lovely, dear." Camino meekly followed Thyme into the back room, leaving me alone with Ruprecht.

"Ruprecht, you knew this was going to happen, didn't you." I said it more as a statement than a question. "I mean, about the police suspecting Camino, even arresting her."

"Yes, I'm afraid I did," Ruprecht said. "I saw it all happening in my scrying mirror."

"What's a scrying mirror?"

"I'll explain it all to you later, Amelia. Right now, I'm concerned that someone tried to frame Camino for Sue's murder. Since they tried once, they might try again."

"You don't think they'll try to, um, well, murder Camino, do you?" I asked, concerned.

Ruprecht shook his head. "I highly doubt that, but it's better to be safe than sorry."

I agreed.

"My main concern, however," Ruprecht continued, "is that Camino might well have inherited something from Sue."

"But I didn't think they were terribly close," I said, "although they were friends. And what does it matter if Camino *did* inherit something?"

Ruprecht scratched his chin. I imagined he really should have a long white beard like Dumbledore or Gandalf, because when he scratched his chin, he looked like he was trying to stroke a non-existent beard.

"Amelia, have you heard what I just said?"

I looked up to see Ruprecht peering at me. "Oh sorry, Ruprecht," I said. "I was just off with the fairies—or wizards, to be precise."

Ruprecht raised one eyebrow, but didn't pursue

the matter. "I just said that Camino told me that she's been invited to the will reading. That means she has indeed inherited something. Let's hope it's only a set of china, or a hat, or a set of cutlery, and nothing more, or else she will have a motive for murder in the eyes of the police."

"Surely Sue left everything of value to her sister," I said.

Ruprecht's eye twitched. "I for one certainly hope you're right, Amelia." His tone was grim.

CHAPTER 18

I swallowed nervously. Thyme seemed strangely calm for somebody who was about to sneak eggs into the hands of a dead woman. Okay, that's a sentence I never want to repeat. We'd been sitting quietly for several minutes as guests slowly poured in and filled the seats, though no speeches or eulogies had begun.

I'd spent most of the previous night thinking up distractions, but had drawn blanks. I'd thought of movies where they do something absurd like pretend to choke, and I'd considered pointing and yelling and hoping everybody would just look, but I realised now it would need to be something a lot more substantial. There was considerable distance between Thyme and Sue's body, and she'd need to get there and back again without anybody noticing.

Thyme had somehow talked me into it, but I couldn't remember how. I understood the idea and realised the importance of finding the murderer, but I wished there was another way to do all of this. I'd never been very good at public events as it was, but causing a distraction seemed like something out of my worst nightmare.

Late last night, I'd given up on ideas and just figured I could improvise. Now, that seemed like the worst idea in the world. I knew I had to do something before anybody got on the stage to give a speech, or they'd have a clear line of sight on Thyme and my distraction would have to be that much more drastic. Doing it while people were still gathering would probably be easier too, but...

"Amelia, if you're going to do something, do it now," Thyme hissed. She was apparently more nervous than she appeared, which made me feel somehow better, though the realization that I had to do something overtly embarrassing dashed any feelings of happiness. I looked over my shoulder, and saw that the doors were closed. All the guests had arrived, and they were about to begin the speeches. I decided that I'd have to do something quickly, but before I could, a man stood up and took the stage. He was quite old, and seemed to have a bit of difficulty speaking.

"Hello, everybody. Thanks for coming. My name is Dyson Webster, and I'm an old friend of Sue's." He spoke softly, making an effort to move his eyes around the room as he did so. "She was a wonderful woman, and we are all sad to see her leave us. As I'm not from these parts, it does me a lot of good to see just how many friends Sue had here. Before we begin, I just wanted to say thank you for that, to everybody that knew her. They say that 'I'm sorry' and 'I apologise' mean the same thing, unless you're at a funeral,"—he paused while everybody laughed—"but I truly am sorry that we didn't have more time to spend with her. She will be missed." He smiled weakly and walked back to his seat. The main speeches were about to start, and I knew this was my last chance.

I remained standing as everybody else sat down, and then walked into the aisle. "Attention, everybody!" I said, and then I choked. I had managed to draw their attention away from Thyme, but I had no idea what to do now. "I, uh..." I stammered. "I just wanted to say, that... Sue was... good. And I am very sad that she has died." Nobody moved or made a sound. After a few seconds that felt like hours, people began to turn back to the front, where I could see Thyme had begun to enact her plan. I needed to buy her a lot more time.

"And," I yelled much too loudly, startling everybody, "before she died, she taught me this, uh, this poem." I saw Ruprecht raise an eyebrow so high that I thought it would probably cause permanent facial damage.

"She told me that she was very proud of learning it, and that it wasn't for everybody, but I felt it was so profound and beautiful that it should be shared." I sighed softly. This was so embarrassing, but I'd come too far to back out now, and it was for a good cause. "So, before the ceremony begins, I'd like you all to hear it."

I was never a very good public speaker, but I was a much worse poet. To make it worse, I'd never had any real practice improvising anything, much less in such a public situation. I thought back to my ancient history lessons in high school. I tried to remember what the Greek poet, Simonides, had said about Leonidas and the Three Hundred who fell at Thermopylae.

I quoted the epitaph:

"Go tell the Spartans passing by
That here obedient to their laws we lie."

There was a collective gasp, and some assorted giggles throughout those gathered.

Thyme signalled to me to continue, so I pushed on. I tried to think of another poem, but in the stress of the moment, I could only remember an ancient prayer for safety at sea. Thyme gestured urgently, so I figured I had no choice but to quote it.

"Mighty sons of Zeus and of Leda,
Be with me now as I leave the Isle of Pelops!
Castor and Polydeuces, be kind and appear to me,
you who wander over the wide earth, over
all the sea's domain on your flying horses,
easily delivering mortals from the terror of
death,
as you fly down to the strong ship's
mast and ride on the cables,
through the dark night."

I thought that was not particularly relevant to Sue's funeral, so I added, "Sue died just like Leonidas and the Three Hundred, and like those ancient Greeks would've died if they hadn't prayed to the gods for safety at sea." I stopped speaking and looked around the room.

Everybody seemed fixated on my bizarre outburst.

I could no longer see Thyme from where I was standing and had no idea if she'd managed her task or not, but I figured I should buy her as much time as I possibly could. I couldn't remember any more poems, so I managed to blurt out some more awkward sentences using all the flowery language and long words I could muster.

I managed to spout a few more incoherent lines, and everybody stared at me in silence. It was so quiet I felt as though I could actually hear my face turning beet red. Someone in the audience coughed softly, and I wanted nothing more than for this moment to end. Someone tapped me on the shoulder and I jumped, spinning around to face them. It was Kayleen.

"Are you done embarrassing yourself?" she yelled at me. "Some of us have places to be after this funeral, so let's move it along." She said it so rudely that I was momentarily stunned. I could see Craig nodding in agreement over her shoulder, although her own husband looked shocked. She then leant in close to me and whispered, calling me some of the rudest names I had ever heard. In fact, some of them I had never even heard. She then pretended to pat me on my shoulder, but pinched me viciously.

I slapped her across the face as hard I could. She crashed backwards into the seats behind her, knocking strangers in every direction. Several people stood up. I knew I'd have to leave. Giving Kayleen a last sour look, I turned and walked outside, hoping Thyme had managed to do her part.

I hugged my arms around myself and sat on the steps of the funeral home's chapel. I'd hugely embarrassed myself, and what I'd done to Kayleen was wrong, even if I felt she deserved it. *People are going to hate me for that*, I thought, *but if Thyme got it done, it was all worth it.* The commotion inside grew suddenly louder as the front door opened, but quieted down again as it closed gently.

"Are you okay?" It was Ruprecht. He sat down next to me and looked out to the horizon.

"I've been a lot better," I admitted. True, I'd also been worse, but I also hadn't ever slapped somebody at a funeral. Hopefully, I wouldn't have to do it again.

"Now, you didn't necessarily handle that in the most elegant fashion, but as far as I could tell, Thyme did her part, so we're that much closer to catching the killer." He smiled warmly at me. "It was selfless of you to embarrass yourself for a good cause like that. It was less selfless to slap that woman across the face, but at least that was for two good causes." He chuckled, and I couldn't help but laugh a little with him.

"I couldn't think of a good one-liner," I admitted with a smile.

Ruprecht turned to me. "A one liner?"

"You know, a line after you do something exciting, like in the movies, or on *Buffy*. I could have said 'Eat this' if I'd hit her with one of my cakes, or I could have said, 'I won't take this sitting down,' and hit her with a chair, or something." I laughed, albeit somewhat hysterically.

Ruprecht chuckled with me. "I think you made your point as it is, to be honest. More importantly, we're much closer to discovering the identity of the killer. I think Sue would have approved of your actions, even if it does lead to a less than ideal reputation around town."

"You think that people are going to hold this against me for long?" I hadn't really had time to process how long people might be upset with me over this, but I realised it could be a very long time.

"No, I don't. Not for long, anyway. Grief

makes people do silly things, and Kayleen is immensely unpopular around town. She's alienated so many people. Plus, we can help steer people away from accusing you of any wrongdoing." He smiled reassuringly.

I smiled back, but I wasn't fully reassured. I could handle the gossip and people being upset with me, but I wasn't sure the business could survive too much of a negative reputation. *This plan had better work*, I thought.

CHAPTER 19

$\mathcal{I}$ was happily filling the glass display cases with various cupcakes in an elegant arrangement, if I do say so myself. I was in a good mood, as Thyme had managed to place the eggs in Sue's hands after all, right before Sue was cremated. Thyme assured me that the murderer would be caught soon. My extreme embarrassment was not for naught, after all. Plus, there had been more customers than usual that morning, and all but one of them had congratulated me heartily for my speech at the funeral. I figured that was code for being happy that I had slapped Kayleen. Of course, physical violence is never the best answer, and I wouldn't have done it if I hadn't had to

157

provide a distraction to help catch a murderer. Anyway, that's my story and I'm sticking to it.

However, my happy mood vanished when Ruprecht walked into the store. My stomach sank. I could tell by the look on his face it was not good news. "What's happened?" I asked him.

"It's Camino," he said. Before I could ask what had happened to her, he pushed on. "Camino is supposed to go to the will reading today, but she refuses to leave her room. I've tried everything to get her out and she just won't leave. She's locked the door, and now she won't even speak to me. I need your help."

"I certainly won't be able to get her to leave her room if you can't, Ruprecht," I said. "You have more influence over her than anyone else does."

Ruprecht rubbed his forehead and all at once looked one hundred years older than he already was. "No, Amelia. I'm afraid I need your help in another matter."

That threw up a big red flag. "No, I won't create another diversion," I said. "Even the thought of it makes me want to be sick. I can't go through anything like that again." I realised I was waving my arms around me, but I really didn't care.

Ruprecht did not hurry to reassure me, which made me even more worried. "We just need someone to impersonate Camino," he said.

I took a deep breath, a very deep breath. "I don't think I heard you quite right," I said slowly. "I thought you said that you needed someone to impersonate Camino, but that would be a crazy thing to say, so I know you couldn't have said it."

Ruprecht's face flushed beet red. "I'm sorry, Amelia. It's either you or Thyme. Camino is supposed to go to the will reading today, and the only other person we know who is going is Barbara. We need to know exactly *who* inherits and precisely *what* they inherit. If Camino inherits more than we think, then the police will have their motive, and it won't look good for Camino."

I tapped my forehead hard. "But Ruprecht, I've already created a diversion, and more than one diversion at that. Everyone said all we had to do was put the eggs in Sue's hands and then the murderer would could confess or whatever, but now you're telling me that I have to impersonate Camino?"

Thyme came into the showroom. "I thought I

heard voices," she said. "What's going on?" She looked from me to Ruprecht and back again.

"It's like this," Ruprecht said, "Camino refuses to leave her room. I don't know whether she's sick or has mentally given up because the strain is too much. But whatever the reason, she refuses to leave her room. We really need to know who inherits. One of you two will have to impersonate Camino and go to the will reading. Anyway, I can't stay here too long; I don't want to leave Camino on her own. I'm quite worried about her."

Thyme and I exchanged glances.

"Don't look at me," I said. "I made a fool of myself at the funeral, creating all those diversions. It's not fair that you'd ask me to impersonate Camino. Besides, I still think it's a crazy idea." I pouted.

"I'd happily go," Thyme said.

I crossed my arms. "There's a 'but' in there, isn't there?"

"Yes, sorry, Amelia, there is." Thyme chuckled. "It really isn't fair that you have to impersonate Camino, but I'm afraid you'll have to. Put it this way. One of us has to impersonate Camino and go to that will reading, and the other one has to bake cupcakes."

I thought it over. "Well, I suppose I don't have any choice," I said forlornly. "But just don't ask me to do anything else. I've gone above and beyond."

Ruprecht smiled. "I know it does sound like a silly idea to impersonate Camino, but she really does need to be present at that will reading. We have to know whether she inherits anything."

"But surely her own lawyer will tell her later anyway," I said.

Ruprecht shook his head. "He wouldn't know what Barbara or anyone else inherited. Not only do we need to know what Barbara inherited, but we also need to know if there is anyone else there who inherits, so we can add them to our suspects list," he said. "We need to find out the major beneficiary of the will, and the sooner we find out, the better. But now we have one more problem, Amelia. We have to make you look and sound like Camino."

"I can't even see how it's going to be possible," Thyme said. I shared her opinion, but I was still sulking about having to impersonate Camino the very day after embarrassing myself at a funeral.

"I've already thought it through," Ruprecht said. "We will get one of Camino's dresses, and Amelia can wear padding under it. She can wear a hat and a veil and say she's in mourning. She can say she has a terrible cold and has laryngitis. Well, perhaps laryngitis is going too far. Just say you have a very bad cold, Amelia, and clutch a bunch of tissues to your face."

I clutched my head. "Has the whole world gone mad?" I exclaimed. "Can you guys hear yourself talk?" I normally wouldn't have spoken to Ruprecht in that way, but the whole idea was absurd. "And is it even legal? I don't want to get thrown into the watch house too, especially given that it doesn't have coffee or even snacks between meals."

"Don't worry yourself about the intricacies of it, Amelia," Ruprecht said. "If you are discovered, then Camino can state that she sent you as her appointee."

But that won't explain why I was impersonating her, I thought, but I kept my mouth shut. I knew a lost cause when I encountered one.

Thyme pulled a face. "Quite honestly, Amelia, I would seriously do it, but there's a lot of baking to be done today. So it's either you bake and end up with burned cakes, or you impersonate Camino."

"Yes, I know; I have no choice in the matter," I said grumpily.

And so, in less than half an hour, I found myself in Camino's house with Mint. She held up a black billowing dress. "Here, put on this dress."

"Are you kidding?" I said. "It's hideous."

"Well, it's not as if you're going on a date," Mint said with a chuckle. "You need to get into character. Just pretend you're acting. You have to impersonate Camino."

I groaned, feeling quite sorry for myself. Mint handed me an oversized bra. "Here, put this on first."

I put it on over my own bra, and it hung off me like a couple of parachutes after they had landed.

Mint doubled over with laughter and fell on the bed. "That's hilarious."

"You're not helping," I said.

Mint was obviously doing her best not to laugh again. She handed me a box of tissues. "Here, stick these down Camino's bra."

"I think I need something more substantial than tissues," I said. "And what are we going to do about my waist?"

Mint handed me two pillows. "We can find

something to tie these around you. What about a curtain cord or something like that?"

After a few minutes of rummaging around, we managed to find a length of curtain cord which Mint tied around me. "Hey, not too tight," I said. "I need to be able to breathe. Plus these pillows are filled with feathers! They're poking into me."

After adjusting the cord, Mint climbed onto a chair and pulled a box from the top of the closet. "Let's look through these hats for something with a veil."

"Surely Camino wouldn't have a hat with a veil," I protested, but no sooner had the words left my mouth than Mint produced a weird looking hat with what looked like turkey feathers sticking out the top. A black veil was attached to it. "I think Camino wore this to the Melbourne Cup one year, back in the day," Mint said. She was barely suppressing her laughter. She stuck it on my head.

"That will look good once I've powdered your hair to match Camino's hair color," she said gleefully.

I looked at myself in the mirror, and it was all I could do not to burst out laughing. "I think I don't look anything like Camino," I said. "Anyway, Barbara has stayed with Camino for a few days and knows what she looks like and how she sounds. How on earth am I expected to get away with this?"

"These will help." Mint handed me a package of support stockings.

"What are these things?" I asked. "They look like murder weapons more than anything else."

"You just put them on," Mint said. "Thankfully your feet are the same size as Camino's."

"How lucky is that," I said with as much sarcasm as I could muster.

Mint stood back to admire her handiwork. "Not too bad, but you'll have to remember to disguise your voice. Luckily that veil is large and thick, and don't forget that they'll be expecting to see Camino. Never in their wildest dreams would they imagine that it would be you impersonating Camino."

I threw up my hands in horror. "I don't think there are enough tissues to stick in the bra, Mint," I said.

"Wait, I have an idea." Mint hurried out of the room, while I pulled on the horrible thick support stockings. Mint return to the room with two oranges. "Here, put these in the bra."

"Are you crazy? I'm not putting those in a bra! They'll be uncomfortable."

Mint shook her head. "They will give you more shape than the tissues will." She handed the oranges to me.

I pushed them into Camino's bra and packed tissues around them. I had to admit that they gave the bra a better shape than the tissues alone. I tightened the shoulder straps, and the oranges sat nicely. They were a little heavy, but they were probably the least of my worries.

Mint handed me something that looked like a cross between a deflated hot air balloon and a tutu. It was white and covered with rows of large frills. I backed away from her, moving behind the bed, and held my hands up in front of me. "You must be joking! There's no way I'm going to wear that. What on earth is it? I've never seen anything like it. It looks like something they wore in Victorian times. You can't make me wear it," I squeaked. "I've never seen Camino wearing it!"

Mint laughed. I could see she was enjoying herself too much. "Of course you haven't seen Camino wearing them," she said. "They're bloomers."

"What on earth are bloomers?" I asked her, "and where on earth do you put them?"

"They're underwear, silly."

I put my hands on my hips. "Great, because if they're underwear, then no one will see them and I don't have to wear them."

"Oh come on, Amelia, they'll pad out the dress. The pillow isn't enough."

"Oh well, in for a penny, in for a pound," I said. I figured I might as well resign myself to the situation. After all, I was pretending to be Camino. The weird clothes and the bizarre underwear would not reflect upon me personally.

Mint giggled and patted the old tapestry seat in front of Camino's dressing table. "Sit."

I dutifully did as I was told. For the next few minutes all I could see was Mint giggling and waving various makeup brushes in front of me. "This is going to look really bad isn't it?" I said.

"Just try to get into character please, Amelia. There's a lot riding on this."

"Easy for you to say," I said, "and come to think of it, why didn't you volunteer for this expedition?"

Mint smirked again. "I tend to get fits of the giggles when I'm nervous," she said. "Grandfather wouldn't let me go in case I gave the game away by giggling."

I knew this wasn't going to end well. When Mint had finished, I said, "Can I look in the mirror now?" I was concerned when I saw a look of fear flash across Mint's face.

"Don't forget that you'll be wearing a veil," she said hurriedly, "and it's a thick veil."

After those words, I hurried to look in the mirror. I stared at the reflection in front of me. I didn't look anything like myself. I was encouraged by that. Perhaps I had half a chance of pulling this off.

CHAPTER 20

I wasn't so confident when Mr Entwistle, the lawyer greeted me. He was elderly and stooped, and I hoped his thick-rimmed glasses were an old prescription. I didn't know how well he knew Camino, if at all, but the whole situation was leaving me nervous indeed. Thankfully, he didn't give my face a second look. His eyes did go straight to my hat feathers, but surely that was to be expected. Barbara was already in the lawyer's office, and no one else but Barbara was there.

I took the only empty seat, next to Barbara, and forced a cough. "Terrible sore throat," I squeaked. "It was so cold in that watch house." Barbara shot me a look. I thought perhaps I shouldn't have alluded to the fact that I, or rather

Camino, had just been arrested for murder. I remembered my father's old saying, "Even a fool appears wise if he's silent." I thought it prudent to take his advice. I spluttered the word, "Laryngitis," and then shut my lips firmly together.

Now if only I could keep my head down and not say anything, and then leave the second it was over, I might be okay. I allowed myself a small sigh of relief. I was glad that Barbara was not focusing on me and that the lawyer was oblivious to everything, having his nose firmly stuck in a folder. I sincerely hoped that Barbara would inherit everything of value, and that Camino wouldn't inherit more than a pair of cotton socks, because then the police would surely not suspect her any longer.

"And so," Mr Entwistle said, "without any further ado, this is the last Will and Testament of Sue Valerie Beckett." He read out several pages, or what seemed like several pages, all in legalese and in a slow, monotone voice. It was all I could do to stay awake. Finally, he got to the interesting bit. "Barbara Bowen is to inherit the remainder of the estate after Camino Abre's portion."

Please let Camino's portion be tiny, I thought.

He droned on. "And so this is what constitutes

Miss Beckett's estate minus the bequest to Mrs Abre." He looked at Barbara over his thick spectacles.

I sat through a good half hour of him droning on and on about the house, the amount of money in Sue's bank accounts—I certainly raised my eyes at that one—and the contents of her house.

As he continued, I grew more and more relieved that there was surely nothing left for Camino to inherit. It looked like the lack of a motive would lead to her soon being in the clear with the police. On the other hand, it was looking more and more like Barbara had a good motive. And I had no idea that one person could own so many things. It made me just want to go home and clean out my closet. The lawyer listed clothes, hats, gloves, shoes, wheelbarrows, shovels. Who knew so many items would be listed in a will? Sue must've been a very methodical person. I wondered if she was an accountant. I also needed a drink of water. I didn't want to ask for one, because I wanted to maintain my cover. The less I spoke, the better off I would be.

"And now to Mrs Abre's inheritance," the lawyer said. He shot me a rare glance.

Please don't let it be much; please don't let it be much, I silently chanted.

The lawyer looked back down at his folder and tapped it with his pen. He spoke in a solemn tone. "This was Mrs Beckett's most prized possession," he said.

My heart sank. What could it be? A Ferrari? An Audi? A BMW?

"In fact, I have it right here," he said, screwing up his face. "Mrs Beckett's instructions were that you were to take it at once, Mrs Abre."

My spirits lifted slightly. It wasn't an expensive car. Although what if it was a valuable antique? Perhaps a priceless painting?

Mr Entwistle leant under his desk and reached for the item. I held my breath. I hoped with all my heart that it was something cheap and only had sentimental value.

The lawyer placed a cage on the table with a flourish. I screamed and jumped to my feet. In the cage was the largest rat I had ever seen. Its nose twitched. It opened its mouth, showing what looked to me like a large pair of fangs. Its eyes were beady and glowing. Well, at least that's how it looked through the thick veil.

My scream must have startled the lawyer, for

he jerked forward, and as he did so, the cage bounced on top of a red leather-bound book, which had the words 'The Rule of Law' embossed in gold. The cage door bounced open, and the rat leaped at me.

I screamed again and jumped, and as I did so, I fell backwards over the chair. My legs flew skyward. Thank goodness I was wearing those bloomers, after all. At any rate, I could see the frills on the bloomers in front of my eyes in full display. Through my upturned legs, I could see Mr Entwistle averting his eyes. The rat chose that moment to run across my face. I screamed and screamed, and the rat darted under a bookcase.

Now that I was rat-free, I tried to pull myself together. I did my best to right myself, but as I struggled to my feet, the oranges fell out of my bra and rolled across the floor. "Vitamin C," I squeaked. "For my sore throat. I've lost my handbag so had to wear them on my person." This time, I didn't need to disguise my voice, given that I had screamed so loudly at the rat.

Thankfully there was now no sign of the rat, and I managed to pull myself to my feet. I felt a little lighter given that the oranges were on the floor. I hoped Mr Entwistle and Barbara didn't notice that a certain part of my person was now smaller than it had been.

Unfortunately, my heavy fall backwards onto the floor had burst the pillows tied around me, and feathers were falling out from under my hideous black dress. I had no idea how to explain that one away, so I just pretended I didn't notice.

I clutched the pillows to me so they wouldn't fall out. "Sore stomach," I squeaked again. "From seeing the rat. I'm allergic to rats."

"I'll have the rat, if that's all right with you, Camino," Barbara said. "Sue and I always kept rats as pets when we were children. Sue must've been mistaken. She told me that you loved rats."

Well, why didn't she leave it to you in the will? I thought. I clutched the deflated pillows and nodded to Barbara. "Thank you, thank you. May I leave now, Mr Entwistle? I feel ill."

"Yes, please do," Mr Entwistle managed to say between sneezes. The room was rapidly filling up with feathers.

CHAPTER 21

*R*uprecht was standing in front of a whiteboard with a thin wooden pointer. It looked like the Elder Wand from Harry Potter, but I wasn't going to say that out loud. In his other hand, he clutched a whiteboard marker. "So, what do we know now?" Without waiting for anyone to answer, he pushed on. "We know that Sue was killed with botulinum; Botox if you will. We also know that Sue had Botox treatment at Simone's the day she died. Now, the police also know that, yet have not charged Simone. Rather, they arrested Camino. What does that tell us?"

I felt like I was back in school. I looked at Thyme and Mint, but no one spoke. Camino was still in her room. Ruprecht had told us that she had been out for meals, but had gone back and locked herself in again. At least we knew she was alive. Ruprecht refused to let her return home until the murderer was safely behind bars.

And so Thyme, Mint, and I were sitting in front of Ruprecht's whiteboard in one of the back rooms at his store. We were all sipping hot cinnamon, orange, and Rooibos tea, and eating an unseemly number of chocolate chip cookies as well as peanut butter fudge cupcakes I had brought from the store. I hadn't baked them, needless to say.

I was the first to speak up. "I'm not too sure," I said with a shrug of my shoulders.

"I suppose it means that the police are very sure that Simone didn't do it?" Thyme ventured.

Ruprecht nodded. "Yes, but they arrested Camino, so we cannot have full confidence in the police." He stretched up his hand and wrote on the whiteboard, 'Suspects.' He underlined the word with a flourish. Underneath it, he wrote, 'Barbara, Simone, Madison, Bob,' and then wrote a question mark. "There must also be a suspect that we have not yet suspected," he said. "It's always good to leave the matter open."

With a scrawl, Ruprecht wrote 'Motive,' and underlined it three times. Under it, he wrote, 'Money, Love, Revenge.' He turned to us. "These are the three main motives for killing someone. If Barbara was the murderer, then her motive was money. If Simone is the killer, then her motive can either be revenge or love. We know it cannot have been money. And if we have an unknown assailant, then we know that their motive was love or revenge. Now, we know that Sue was having an affair with Bob, Madison's husband. That means that if Bob or Madison killed Sue, then their motive was love or revenge, maybe even both. Now where does that leave us?"

"If you don't mind me saying so," I said. "I thought the murderer would come forward and reveal him or herself. Isn't that why we went to all the trouble of putting eggs in Sue's hands?"

Ruprecht laid down his pointer and stepped forward. "Amelia, I have always tried to tell you that practical aspects go hand in hand with spell work. As I have always said to you, if someone is looking for a job, that person not only does a spell for a job but must also do the practical work of applying for jobs. They cannot rely on the spell alone. The two go hand-in-hand. We must take

177

practical measures as well, and then, rest assured, the murderer will reveal him or herself."

"Oh," I said in a small voice.

"Amelia, I have a job for you."

I stood up. "No!" I screeched. "Please don't make me. I can't go through it again. It was bad enough having to make up a poem on the spot, and then I had to impersonate Camino!" I shuddered at the memories. "What is it now?"

Ruprecht did his best to stop laughing, or so it seemed to me. "Nothing as bad as that this time, Amelia," he said. "I overheard you talking to Simone at the Customer Appreciation Night and you mentioned you would make an appointment soon."

I wondered where he was going with this. "Yes. I'm overdue to have my eyebrows and eyelashes tinted and my eyebrows waxed."

"Well," Ruprecht said, "how would you feel about making an appointment with Simone as soon as possible?"

I pulled a face. "What's the catch?"

Ruprecht smiled. "Nothing, really. There must be some reason that the police didn't arrest Simone. Just ask questions and snoop around. You don't need to go over the top. Just play it by ear. If beauty therapists are anything like hairdressers, I imagine that they talk a lot."

"Yes, that's right," I said. "I suppose that won't be so bad. I was meaning to make an appointment soon, anyway. What sort of things do you want me to ask her?"

He shrugged. "You could ask her if she's had any robberies there lately, and perhaps ask her if anyone has requested to buy Botox from her. I'm sure it would be illegal for her to sell it, but it won't hurt to ask her if anyone has made such a request."

"I suppose I could do that." I couldn't see any harm in asking simple questions while I was having my regular appointment, but that didn't stop the horribly apprehensive feeling gnawing at the pit of my stomach. Still, I couldn't see what could go wrong.

As it turned out, Simone was able to fit me in that very afternoon. My eyebrows and eyelashes had both faded, and my eyebrows did need a good waxing, but knowing I was going there with an ulterior motive made me most nervous.

"Dark brown, as usual?" Simone asked as she ushered me into the treatment room.

"Yes, please," I said. "Sorry my eyebrows are so overdue."

"No worries," Simone said. "That's what I'm here for. It might just hurt a bit more than usual."

"That's okay," I said. "I never find eyebrows are too painful, anyway."

While Simone was applying the hot wax to my eyebrows, I kept quiet. I didn't want to make her annoyed while she was armed with hot wax.

As soon as she ripped off the wax, she started applying the tint to my eyebrows and eyelashes. I took my opportunity to speak. "That's a terrible thing that happened to Camino, isn't it?" I said.

"You mean being arrested for Sue's murder," Simone said.

"Yes. You don't think she did it, do you?" I asked her.

Simone paused to look at me. "No, of course not!" she exclaimed.

I pushed on. "Did the police question you?"

Simone started applying the tint again. "Yes, they gave me the third degree," she said. "I was very worried, given that Sue was poisoned with Botox. The police came and took samples from me. In fact, they searched the whole place and my home as well. It was an absolute nightmare."

"Just as well they didn't think you were the murderer, then, given that you had the murder weapon in your possession." I was careful to make my tone even.

Simone did not appear to be offended. "Yes, they actually told me that because Sue had Botox treatment every three months, and had done so for years, that the murderer would have known that, and that's why the murderer poisoned her with Botox on the very same day."

"Do they know how the murderer got the Botox?" I asked her. "Have you had any robberies or anything like that lately?"

"No," Simone said. "Of course, the police asked me that, too. The police told me that Botox is easy to get in Mexico."

"Mexico!" I exclaimed. "So that's why they were asking everyone if they had been to Mexico."

Simone shrugged. "I suppose so."

"Has anyone ever tried to buy Botox from you?" I asked her.

"No," Simone said. "Of course I wouldn't sell it to anyone, but no one has ever asked me."

"So the police think someone bought the Botox in Mexico?" I asked her.

"No idea," she said. "Now, Amelia, this tint has

181

to stay on for fifteen minutes, as usual. Remember not to open your eyes or squint, or the tint will get into your eyes and sting. I have to leave the room for a few minutes because my husband's coming in to do the books today." She didn't sound pleased at the prospect, and I wondered about the state of their relationship.

I lay in the dark—the dark caused by my eyes being tightly shut—listening to what was meant to be soothing music. However, my overactive imagination sent me visions of Simone slipping in and stabbing me. I was terrified lying there, having my eyes firmly shut. What if Simone was the murderer? I had just asked her questions. What if that alarmed her and she decided to do away with me? I could hardly defend myself when I was lying on a beauty therapy table with my eyes shut. I broke out in a cold sweat. I tried to calm my breathing so I could hear if anyone was in the room with me.

After what seemed an age, I heard the door open. "Who's there?" I said in alarm.

"It's only me," Simone's voice said. "Are you all right?"

"Oh yes, I'm fine," I lied. "Is it time to take the tint off yet?"

"Is it stinging? I have a bowl of warm water with me."

To my relief, Simone removed the excess tint from my eyebrows and my eyelashes without stabbing me once.

Emboldened by my relief over that fact, I thought I should get in a few more questions before the appointment was over. "Simone, you didn't have anything against Sue, did you?"

"What do you mean?" Simone said abstractly as she applied some soothing cream to the area under my eyebrows.

"Oh, nothing at all," I said. I mean, she would hardly admit it to me, would she?

"Did the police say if Sue was injected with Botox, or was it slipped into her food or drink?" I asked her.

"I wouldn't have a clue," Simone said. "They were the ones asking all the questions. I can tell you, Amelia, I'm so glad that I wasn't the one they arrested. Oh sorry, I don't mean I was glad they arrested Camino, but I was sure glad they didn't arrest me. I mean, after all, I was the one with the Botox. I thought that put me in a very bad position."

I agreed. "Whoever the murderer was, they

must've wanted it to look like it was you, or Camino."

Simone appeared to have lost interest in the conversation. "Now, Amelia, can I book you in for four weeks' time? You really can't let your eyebrows get into such a state again."

"Sure," I said. I followed Simone out into her desk area, where she booked me in and handed me an appointment card. I noticed a surly man sitting behind the counter. He kept glaring at me. It finally dawned on me who he was. "Hello Victor," I said. It was Simone's husband, of course, the owner of the conference centre. For a moment, I had forgotten that they were married. I said goodbye to Simone and was about to leave, but Victor spoke up.

"Can I have a word with you, Amelia?" he asked. "Outside."

I nodded. "Of course." I figured that he wanted to speak with me about catering and cupcakes.

When we stepped outside, Victor's demeanour became threatening. He loomed over me, and I involuntarily took a step backwards.

"So, Amelia, how well did you know Sue Beckett?"

I felt defensive, and I didn't know why. "Well, I met her for the first and only time at Camino's that night, playing Clue."

Victor snarled at me. His lips peeled back, showing his teeth, and an ugly vein popped out in his neck. He looked for all the world like a wild animal. "Are you telling me the truth?"

"I am. Why do you ask? I don't understand why you're asking me this." I tried to act as if I were not feeling threatened.

He did not respond, but simply asked me another question. "Sue Beckett and your friend, Camino Abre, were very close, weren't they?"

I took another step back. "I don't think they especially were. I met Sue for the first time that night, as I just told you, and I do see a lot of Camino. I had never seen the two of them together before."

"I overheard you asking my wife some very nosy questions," he said. "I think you'd be better off not sticking your nose into things that don't concern you."

"Are you threatening me?"

"I'm just telling you to mind your own business, or someone else will mind it for you, missy." He shook his finger in my face.

CHAPTER 22

"*I*s everything all right here?"

I swung around to see Alder hurrying up to us.

Victor spun on his heel and ducked back into the building, slamming the door behind him.

"What was that all about?" Alder asked me.

"I'm pretty sure Victor just threatened me," I said. "He said he overheard me asking his wife, Simone, questions. I was just in there having my eyebrows done."

"And they look very nice indeed." Alder was being charming, as usual.

I smiled, and my breathing returned to normal —sort of. Victor had given me quite the fright, but

Alder raised my breathing and heart rates for an entirely different reason.

Alder frowned. "Victor has an unfortunate personality. I've never heard anyone with a good word for him. And what questions did you ask Simone?"

"We all figured that the police must've had a good reason for not arresting Simone, given that Sue was murdered with botulinum, and Simone does Botox treatments. She told me that she'd given Sue Botox treatments on a regular basis, and I asked her if the police let on whether Sue was killed with a Botox injection or whether botulinum was slipped into her food or drink. I also asked her if anyone had ever attempted to buy Botox from her."

"Well, I'm impressed," Alder said. "Maybe I should hire you."

I smiled again. "Maybe you should, but everyone knows I'm just the most fabulous baker." We both laughed at that one.

"And what information did you get from her?"

"Nothing at all, really. She said no one had ever tried to buy Botox from her, and she said she had nothing against Sue. She said Sue religiously came to her for a Botox treatment every three months."

Alder nodded. "That's interesting," he said. "Anyway, I was coming to see you."

"You were?" I hoped I didn't sound as ridiculously happy as I was. The chemistry between us was so strong that I could almost hear the air crackling. I hoped it wasn't my imagination. I hoped Alder felt it too, at least in some measure.

He nodded. "Yes. What are your plans for tonight?"

My plans for that night had been to hurry over to *Glinda's* and tell the others what Simone had said, and how I had felt threatened by Victor. Of course, since I was in my right mind—although some would contest that—I would hardly say that to Alder. Instead I said, "Nothing."

"Would you like to have dinner with me tonight?" he asked.

I forced myself to hesitate for a moment. I didn't want to look too keen. After what seemed to me to be the right interval, I said, "Yes, that would be lovely."

"Is now too soon for dinner?"

"No, now would be just perfect," I gushed and then silently chided myself.

"Would you like to go to the Italian restaurant?"

"Yes, I love Italians." Wait, did I just say that? I'd meant to say 'Italian.' Alder was Italian, so I hoped he didn't read anything into my remark.

"I have some interesting, although disturbing, news I want to share with you. I would tell the others, too, but of course that's impossible, given that they don't trust me."

"Oh." I was crestfallen. This must be a business dinner, after all. I hoped my disappointment didn't show on my face.

There weren't many restaurants in Bayberry Creek. I had only been to the Italian restaurant once or twice. There were two pubs that had good restaurants (as did most Aussie pubs), one motel with a good restaurant, and two Chinese restaurants, one of them good. The Italian restaurant was next door to my favourite coffee shop.

We walked straight there. I thought again that Alder smelled like an old witch—in a good way that is—like ancient white sage. I had only been to Britain once, but Alder was someone I would expect to find there, under a tree of his namesake, or under ivy, or perhaps at a gate to a fairy grove.

He reminded me of one of those people of legend who would appear to someone and ask them to accompany him back into an underground cavern to meet the queen of the fairies.

It was an intimate atmosphere. I noticed that fact as soon as I walked through the door. It was old and quaint, with walls in mismatched colours. One wall was a kind of a cross between burgundy and salmon, while the other wall appeared to be mustard with a gold paint effect overlay, one of the paint effects that was popular late last century. Paintings and prints covered most of the mustard-coloured wall, leaving not much paint to be seen. There appeared to be no rhyme or reason to the paintings. On closer inspection, I saw they all had prices marked on them. Along another wall were many books haphazardly stacked along old wooden bookshelves. The books all appeared to be old, leather-bound and decaying. From them, an ancient musty scent emanated and pervaded the entire room.

Still, all of that only served to add to the cozy atmosphere. There were dimmed, yellowed lights over the tables, and the only bright light came in the form of two low-hanging pendant lights over the service area. In fact, they were so low that the tallest staff member had to keep ducking to avoid hitting his head on them.

The tablecloths likewise were mismatched. Some were bright red and white checks, while others were solid navy blue. There was one white one, and the rest looked like something an ancient granny had stored in a chest in an attic. On the other hand, the chairs all matched each other. They appeared to be from the Edwardian era, and looked somewhat uncomfortable. All around the room were thin wooden lampstands with shades adorned with fringes. These reminded me of lamps in bordellos in old western movies.

The tall waiter greeted Alder enthusiastically, seizing his hand and shaking it vigorously. He showed us to a table at the back of the room, the most dimly-lit table in the room. A pang of jealousy assaulted me, and I wondered if Alder was in the habit of bringing women here.

The waiter asked us what we would like to drink, and promised to return promptly with water. I looked at the menu, feeling awfully nervous being here alone with Alder. For some reason, I was even more nervous than when I had been alone with him in his house.

When the waiter left, Alder leant forward. He

looked to me like a sexy vampire in one of those movies where the vampire is always portrayed as dashing rather than a bloodthirsty beast.

"Now the reason I wanted to speak with you," he said, "apart from wanting your company, is that Frida McGeever came to see me today. Do you know her?"

I was puzzled. "No, I've never heard of her."

"She has that little knitting and crochet shop next to the hairdresser in the Main Street."

"Well, that's why I've never heard of her," I said. "My knitting is on the same level as my baking."

Alder laughed. I could barely take my eyes from him. He had to be the most attractive man I'd ever seen. "To come straight to the point, she came to see me to tell me that Sue Beckett had been blackmailing her."

I had no idea what that was all about. This was all getting stranger and stranger. I felt like I had fallen into a chapter of *Alice in Wonderland*.

I was keen to hear what he had to say next. Just then the waiter returned and asked us if we would need more time to see the menu. We both said that we would. I hadn't so much as looked at the menu yet. To my disappointment, instead of telling me what Frida McGeever had told him, Alder left me in suspense while he perused the menu.

To make matters worse, the waiter hovered over us. For that reason, I chose the first thing I saw that looked okay, cauliflower with pine nuts and mint. The menu described it as served with roasted Dutch carrots sprinkled with toasted pine nuts and coated with cashew cream.

I sure hope it tasted okay. Alder ordered the tempura saltbush. That sounded a little adventurous to me; it sounded like something that Bear Grylls would eat.

At least the waiter left at that point, so I waited for Alder to continue his story.

"I'll have to give you some background information," he said. "Some months ago, Frida's husband, Tom, employed my services to ascertain whether Frida was having an affair." He held up his hand. "The name of my client, needless to say, is confidential?" He said it as a question rather than a statement.

I nodded, wondering where all this was going. "Of course," I said hurriedly.

"As I said, Tom came to see me to ask me to look into whether Frida was having an affair. He didn't have any suspects in mind, but he said she often hung up her phone when he entered the room and she was often home late. In fact, one time she said she was staying overnight with a certain friend of hers, but then he later found out that the friend was in another state at the time."

"And she was having an affair?"

Alder nodded. "Yes, she sure was, and with two different men."

"Well," I said. "Bayberry Creek seems like such a sleepy little town. I had no idea such things went on here."

Alder raised one eyebrow and looked at me from under his long eyelashes. "You'd be surprised! Anyway, I gave the job to Sue, as I always did. As I've told you, my main work is insurance fraud, but I don't turn down any cases if I can help it. I used to outsource the adultery cases to Sue."

I nodded again, suspicions forming in my mind.

He pressed on. "Sue reported back to me that Frida was not having an affair. I thought no more of it. Frida came to see me today to tell me that Sue had been blackmailing her. Sue had threatened to tell Frida's husband exactly what she was up to. Sue had plenty of photographic evidence of Frida and her lovers."

I gasped. "You're kidding! And did she think you were in on it, too? Was she angry with you?"

Alder shook his head. "Sue made it very clear to Frida that I had no involvement at all, and that Frida was not to tell me."

I tapped my chin. "So, are you thinking what I'm thinking? That Sue blackmailed the wrong person, and that's why she was killed?"

Alder nodded. "Yes. I've already been to the police with this information."

"I wonder who else she blackmailed?"

"I've given the police all the adultery cases I gave Sue since I moved back to Bayberry Creek," Alder said. "I'm obviously especially suspicious of the ones that she said were not adultery."

"Were there many of those?"

Alder rubbed his forehead. "Too many, given the law of averages. In fact, I should have been suspicious of that, but it didn't occur to me that Sue might be blackmailing people. I think it's fair to assume that Frida wasn't the only one she was blackmailing."

At that point the waiter appeared and, in front of Alder, placed what looked like half dead stalks of kale on a piece of paper, as well as a slice of lemon and three blobs of something in a pleasant shade of orange. In front of me he placed a meal that looked far more attractive: a large chunk of cauliflower, with pine nuts and mint leaves. I did not see any roasted carrots, unless they were the burned-looking crispy things on top of the cauliflower. It somehow reminded me of my own cooking, and that was not a good thing.

The waiter poured us each a glass of wine, and then left. Alder took a bite of his food, so I followed suit. It was absolutely delicious. Even the burned looking carrots tasted sublime.

"Is it all right if I tell my friends?" I asked. "I know you said I couldn't, but I really think I should."

Alder rubbed his chin. "All right, then."

"Thanks."

Alder frowned and appeared to hesitate before speaking. "Now there's something personal I need to tell you."

My stomach churned. I wondered what was coming next.

"Remember we talked about someone working magic against you and your friends?"

I nodded. "It's hardly something I'd forget."

"I'm afraid to say this, but whoever it is, is now focusing solely on you, and is focusing hard."

I thought it over. "Could it be Victor, Simone's husband? I was actually scared of him, until you showed up earlier."

"I doubt it, but I can't be sure. It could be anyone." Alder laid his knife and fork on the table and looked at me. "If it was someone obvious, then I would have already ascertained the identity of the person."

"Am I in danger?" I asked him.

"I'm afraid I have no way of knowing that, either," he said. "All I know is that someone is working magic against you. Now Amelia, about dessert..."

At that point my phone rang. I reached for it to switch it off.

"I don't mind if you take that," Alder said.

My face fell at his words. I looked at the caller ID: Thyme. As I swiped my thumb across the screen to answer it, I wondered what Alder had been about to say about dessert. Was he going to suggest that we have dessert back at his place? Was he going to suggest that we should forego dessert altogether? Or was he going to recommend a certain dessert? I would never know.

"Hi, Thyme," I said.

Thyme's tone was urgent. "Amelia, where are you?"

Just as I was wondering how to answer that, mercifully she spoke again. "You have to come home in a hurry!"

CHAPTER 23

I hastily—and regretfully—apologised to Alder, and left the restaurant. Thyme wasn't one to overreact, so I knew the situation was likely serious. But whatever could the problem be? After all, the house could well and truly look after itself.

With anticipation, I drove the short distance to my house. When I got there, I could see Thyme with someone on the front porch, but I couldn't make out who it was. I parked the car on the street, and hurried down my pathway. I recognised Kayleen when I was halfway along the path. I could also hear her yelling.

"What's going on here?" I said. "Kayleen, what on earth are you doing at my house?"

She didn't answer, but simply glared at me.

"I caught her trying to put a poppet under your potted plant," Thyme said.

Kayleen pouted and shook the poppet at me. It had pins sticking out of it, and it had been dressed to look like me. "Why is the poppet holding a lump of charcoal?" I asked her.

"The course said I had to make it lifelike, you idiot," Kayleen said. "You should know that, since you're a witch. And I tried to make it look like you, so I thought I should add some burned food to represent everything you burn. Craig told me how many times you set stuff on fire with your baking. In fact, he told me that when we were…"

Thyme and I both held up our hands. "Too much information!" Thyme said.

"Eew!" I added.

Kayleen put her hands on her hips. "Anyway, I think it's a good likeness of you. You see if you can do better!"

"Hang on a minute. What course is this?" I asked her.

Kayleen looked at me as if I were particularly stupid. "Well, obviously the hexing course I did. It was online. It was twenty percent off if I signed up that day. I thought it was a bargain."

Thyme and I exchanged glances. I took a moment to process the information. "So, Kayleen, are you telling me that you enrolled in an online hexing course to put a curse on me?"

Kayleen smiled. "Yes, and it was a bargain, and even if it hadn't been, it was well worth it! I made poppets of all of you." She swept her hand from me to Thyme, but I assume she meant to include Ruprecht, Camino, and Mint.

"Why would you do a thing like that?" Thyme asked her.

"Well, you're all witches, and all witches should burn in hell."

"What makes you think we're witches?" Thyme asked through gritted teeth.

Kayleen scoffed at her. "Don't try to deny it! Only witches buy things like you all do. How stupid do you think I am?"

"Is that a serious question?" I asked her. Thyme elbowed me in the ribs.

Kayleen shook the poppet at me. "I know you're witches," she said smugly. "Don't forget, I'm the one who delivers your mail. You buy things with pentagrams on them. You buy things called Fast Luck Oil, Money Drawing Powder, Van Van Oil, Protection Incense, and you buy little cauldrons and even crystal skulls. I'm not stupid."

"It's illegal to look in our mail," I said. "And witchcraft is simply a spiritual practice. It's nothing like the Hollywood version of witches. It's not as if witches eat children, or anything like that."

Kayleen, for the first time in our conversation, looked deathly afraid. She backed away and held the poppet in front of her. "I know you eat children!" she said. "I read it in *Hansel and Gretel*."

"But that's just a fairytale," Thyme said. "It's not even true."

"You can't fool me!" Kayleen said. She reached into her pocket and threw some dust at us.

"What's that?" I asked her.

Kayleen turned red. "Oh, I meant to throw it on myself. It's Invisibility Powder, to make you not notice me."

"It's a bit late for that," I said. "We've already noticed you. Anyway, why did you do this while it's still daylight? Shouldn't you have done it after dark, when I was asleep, like any half-way decent criminal would do?"

"Don't give her any ideas," Thyme said.

Kayleen pursed her lips, and clutched the poppet to her chest. "I saw you going into the

Italian restaurant with that busybody, Alder Vervain," she said. "So I knew the coast was clear."

Thyme swung to face me. "What? Is she telling the truth? Were you having dinner with Alder Vervain?"

"Yes," I admitted. "I'll tell you all about it later."

Thyme looked as if she wanted to protest, but mercifully did not.

Kayleen walked over to me and stuck her face close to mine. "I'm going to have you charged for slapping me at the funeral." Her tone was belligerent.

I put my hands on my hips. "You can't do that, Kayleen. It was self defence. You pinched me first."

Kayleen looked a little taken aback, but recovered quickly. "No one saw me pinch you," she protested.

"I saw you pinch her," Thyme said.

Kayleen hesitated.

"And Kayleen, do you know that it's a Federal offence to open and look through someone's mail?" I continued. "It's even worse that you're the mail delivery lady."

Kayleen huffed. "I most certainly did not look through anyone's mail!"

"You just told us both that you did," Thyme said. "In fact, you gave us a long list of things that you found inside our parcels. We're both witnesses to that."

Kayleen's response was to stick out her tongue. "I can do whatever I like. I can have you charged if I want to!"

"Well, see how far you get with that," Thyme said. "You won't be the mail delivery lady any longer once we tell the government that you admitted looking through our mail."

Kayleen visibly paled. "You won't, will you?"

"No, not if you don't charge me with slapping you," I said.

"Okay then. But I will still hex you!" Kayleen then called me a series of names that made my face turn beet red, and walked down the porch steps.

I was furious. Kayleen above all else, had ruined my dinner with Alder. "You had better not try to do any more curses against us, Kayleen," I said, "or I'll..."

Kayleen turned up her face and walked back up the steps to me. She stuck her face inches from mine. "You'll do what, Miss Smarty Pants?"

I thought for a moment, but nothing inventive came to me, so I said the first thing that came to mind. "I'll turn you into a toad, and you'll get a large wart on the end of your nose. See if Craig finds you attractive then!"

Kayleen snorted rudely. "You can't turn anyone into frogs! That's impossible. How stupid do you think I am?"

"On a scale of one to ten?" I asked her. "Anyway, you were right, Kayleen."

Kayleen appeared quite taken aback at my admission. "I was? What about?"

"That Thyme and I are witches," I said. "I didn't want to admit it to you, but you are so clever that I had no choice." Kayleen smirked, but my next words wiped the smirk off her face.

"And it's very easy for powerful witches to turn people into toads."

I was satisfied to see a look of doubt flicker across Kayleen's face.

"You're making this up," she said hopefully.

"Well, you tried to hex us, didn't you?" Thyme said. "If you believe in hexes, and you believe that we are witches, then you must know that we can turn people into toads, complete with large warts on the ends of their noses."

Kayleen's hand flew to her face. "What?" she croaked.

Thyme looked at me. "Did you hear that? Kayleen's voice was croaky and we haven't even started the spell yet."

Kayleen backed away from us. "You wouldn't!"

"Just make sure you stop hexing us right now," I said firmly, "or you will soon wake up to see a giant wart on the end of your nose."

"And you will start to turn green, and hop," Thyme added.

With that, Kayleen threw the poppet at me and sprinted down the path.

CHAPTER 24

My relief at seeing Kayleen flee from my house was short lived. Thyme swung around to face me. "So, you were having dinner with Alder?"

I crossed my arms. "Yes, I was. Thyme, I like him and I trust him. And don't forget, the house likes him."

"Yes, but the house has allowed murderers inside for its own purpose, if you'll recall." Thyme crossed her arms, too.

"Thyme, can't you just trust me on this? And I really do like him."

Thyme hesitated and then let out a long sigh. "Okay, but don't say I didn't warn you. If you really want to date him, then I'll try not to say anything about it."

"Well, I'm not exactly dating him," I said. "He just asked me out to dinner to tell me…" I slapped myself on my head. "Oh, I haven't even had a chance to tell you! There's lots to tell you. Anyway, come on inside, and I'll tell you everything."

As soon as we walked inside, we were met by Hawthorn and Willow complaining loudly that they hadn't been fed. I hurried down the hallway and put the low-cal cat food in their bowls, stroked them both, and then turned to Thyme. "Finally, some peace," I said. "Would you like a cup of tea or some wine?"

"Yes, please, some wine would be lovely, thanks. Red or white, I don't care. Whatever's open."

I pulled some Chardonnay out of the fridge and poured us each a glass. "Come into the living room, and I'll fill you in."

Soon I was telling Thyme that I hadn't discovered any good information from Simone, and that I had felt threatened by her husband, Victor.

"I guess we won't be getting any business from

his conference centre then," Thyme said with a chuckle.

I groaned. "Oh no, I hadn't even thought of that! Anyway, while Victor was speaking with me, Alder turned up."

"How convenient," Thyme said dryly. "Your knight in shining armour."

I shook my finger at her. "You promised you'd be good!"

Thyme just shrugged and took a big sip of her wine.

"And now for the good part. Alder told me that a woman came to see him today, a woman by the name of Frida McGeever. Do you know her?"

"Of course I do. Doesn't everyone? She has that little knitting shop in the main street."

I nodded. "Well, you'll never believe what she told Alder. She told him that Sue Beckett had been blackmailing her."

Thyme's eyebrows shot up, but she didn't speak.

I pushed on. "Okay, now, apparently Alder's main business is insurance fraud, and when he used to get adultery cases, he'd pass them over to Sue. Frida's husband, Tom, employed Alder to see if his wife was having an affair. Alder put Sue on the case, and she reported back to Alder that Frida wasn't having an affair. Meanwhile, Sue started blackmailing Frida."

Thyme's mouth was hanging open in amazement. "So Sue had a racket going?"

"Apparently so. Alder put together a list of all the adultery cases he's had since he came back to Bayberry Creek and took it to the cops today."

"Well then, *there* is the motive for murder!" Thyme exclaimed excitedly. "I'll bet you anything it was one of those adultery cases. Sue was blackmailing the murderer, and the murderer finally had enough of it."

I put my wine glass down on the table. "Yes, it sure seems that way to me."

"See, I told you putting those eggs in Sue's hands would catch the murderer," Thyme said gleefully.

"That hasn't exactly happened yet, Thyme," I pointed out.

"The wheels are turning," Thyme said, waving her hand at me.

I was doubtful. "If you say so."

Thyme looked at her watch. "Gotta run. Ruprecht wants me to take a turn at minding Camino."

"Why does Camino need minding?" I asked her.

"She keeps trying to go back to her home, and Ruprecht says that could be dangerous. He wants her to stay there until the murderer's apprehended."

"So you have to make sure she doesn't make a run for it?"

Thyme laughed. "Yes, that's about the gist of it. Would you like to come?"

I thought it over for a minute, but decided against it. "No, thanks all the same. I've had enough excitement for one day. I think I'll have a long, hot bubble bath and then fall asleep on the couch watching TV."

Thyme stood up. "Well, if you change your mind, just turn up. Ruprecht won't mind. In fact, he'd be delighted."

I assured her that I would. As soon as Thyme left, I went into my bathroom. I admired the claw foot, roll top bathtub every time I walked in the bathroom. It was deep, and as it was made of cast iron, it held the heat nicely. No more having to run hot water at intervals while having a long bath. I poured a generous splash of chocolate and vanilla bubble bath into the running water.

I hopped in the tub surrounded by abundant chocolate-scented bubbles. Great, now I had a terrible chocolate craving. And trust Kayleen to ruin my dinner with Alder. And what had he been going to say about dessert? I shook my head. "You're only being fanciful," I said aloud to myself. "He was just going to ask you what you wanted for dessert."

As soon as I spoke, Willow and Hawthorn appeared. Every time I spoke to myself in the house, they thought I was offering them more food —don't ask me why.

After I got out of the bath and towelled myself dry, I reached for the onesie that Camino had given me as a gift only recently. Then I remembered that Alder had come to the house and found me in it as well as wearing a hideous facial mask. I haven't worn a facial mask since, although I had worn the onesie on several occasions.

The onesie reminded me of Alder and my pre-empted dinner, so I put the onesie aside. The night was still young, so I put on jeans and a T-shirt, and went to find something to watch on TV.

I threw myself back on the couch, and the cats jumped on top of me, sending cat hair flying in all directions. "I don't know where all this hair comes from," I said to them. "I brush you enough, but there's a never ending supply." I reached for the remote, but just as I did so, Jamie Oliver came on.

"Not Jamie Oliver again!" I said to the house. "Don't get me wrong. I like Jamie Oliver, but I don't like watching him twenty-four hours a day, seven days a week. If I promise never to bake again in this house, will you let me watch something else?"

The house turned up the volume by way of answer. I groaned. "It's not going to help," I protested. "I'll never learn to bake. I truly do know the theory—it's just that it doesn't work for me."

There was no response. I leant back on the couch, resigned to watching Jamie Oliver. It could be worse. I was really getting interested in Jamie Oliver listing the ways to use stale bread, when there was a knock at the door.

Who could it be? Had Camino escaped? Had Thyme come back to talk me into going to Ruprecht's? There was only one way to find out.

I dragged myself off the couch and walked to the door. I flung it open.

There was Alder standing on the doorstep. My first thought was that I was glad I wasn't wearing the onesie. My second thought was that he was holding a bag with the restaurant logo.

"Hi, Alder," I said, trying to keep my voice from shaking. He always had that effect on me.

He held up the bag. "Since you ran off like Cinderella, I thought I should bring the dessert to you."

"Don't you mean the shoe?" As soon as I said it, I wished I hadn't, as it implied that I thought he was the handsome prince. Of course, that is exactly what I did think, but I didn't want him to know it. "Would you like to come inside?" I asked him.

"I'd love to, but maybe next time." He handed me the bag.

I looked inside it and saw that there was only one dessert. My face fell. When I had seen him at the door, I assumed he was bringing dessert for both of us.

"I hope you like chocolate coffee roulade?"

"It sounds wonderful," I said, taking the bag from him. Just as I did so, Hawthorn and Willow ran out, attracted no doubt, by the sound of the rustling bag. I suppose it sounded like a bag of cat food being opened. They ran in front of me and knocked me onto Alder.

The two of us rolled down the stairs together, and came to a rest at the bottom of the porch stairs, with Alder landing on top of me.

"Are you hurt?" he asked.

"No." I in fact had no idea if I was hurt. Usually if I had been thrown from a horse or had fallen from a tree, I would move all my limbs gingerly to see if anything was broken. I could hardly do that now, given the circumstances.

Alder made no attempt to lift himself off me. He was so close I could feel his breath on my mouth. Our eyes locked. The world seemed to stand still. For a moment I thought, hoped, he would kiss me, but then my phone rang, breaking the moment.

Alder scrambled off me, and held out his hand to help me up. He nodded and then disappeared down the path almost as fast as Kayleen had.

I sighed and answered my phone. It was Ruprecht. "I think you shouldn't stay there alone tonight," he said. "I don't have a good feeling about it. Please come over and we'll discuss it."

CHAPTER 25

Thyme met me at the front door of Glinda's. "I'm so glad you came. Ruprecht's been stressing. He got upset after he spent time with his scrying mirror. He thinks it's dangerous for you to be in your house at night. He's called all of us here, and now he wants us all to stay overnight."

"Bummer! Why didn't you tell me before I came? I haven't brought my pyjamas or a change of clothes."

"I'm so sorry, Amelia. Never mind, Camino has plenty of changes of clothes, and onesies." She laughed.

I let out a long sigh. "Well, I suppose I could wear a onesie tonight," I said. *Now that Alder won't be seeing me*, I added silently. I thought back to that moment. We had been about to kiss, of that I was certain. Ruprecht's timing left a lot to be desired.

"So you can stay?"

I nodded. "At least I've already fed the cats," I said. And I had given them a special treat for tripping me up and into Alder.

Thyme ushered me into the back room behind Glinda's and then through a large oak door. It opened to reveal a house. At that moment, I realised I had never been in Ruprecht's residence before; I had only been in his shop, and the rooms behind the shop. Ruprecht's residence looked similar to his store. I still felt as if I were in a scene from Harry Potter, more particularly in Dumbledore's office. The scent of Nag Champa incense was pungent throughout.

Strangely, the living room encompassed an internal courtyard, in the centre of which was a tinkling fountain that appeared to be of ancient Roman design. There was a large telescope next to a huge sundial in the courtyard, and the many tables in the living room were covered with puzzling instruments. Ruprecht came forward to greet me.

"Amelia, I'm so glad you could make it," he

said wiggling his eyebrows up and down. "My scrying mirror has given me cause for concern. I, for one, would feel much better if all of you would stay here every night. I feel the danger is only in the night time. I think you'll be safe to return in daylight hours. This, of course, is just until the murderer is caught, and I feel that will happen very soon now."

"Do you really think those eggs will work?" I asked him.

"With all certainty," Ruprecht said. "That is an ancient African tradition carried into modern hoodoo. It will work."

I made to respond, but my attention was pulled to a strange looking object on an old walnut table. "What on earth is that?" I asked him.

"An armillary sphere."

I had no idea what an armillary sphere was, and I crossed to look at it. It was a fascinating metal object consisting of concentric circles with an arrow sticking through the middle. Ruprecht followed me to the table. "It's actually a model of objects in the sky. This one is centred on the earth but some are centred on the sun. It represents lines of celestial longitude and latitude."

I looked at a strange golden disc sitting in a

wooden block. "Does that do the same sort of thing?"

Ruprecht nodded. "Yes, that's an astrolabe. It's actually an ancient astronomical computer."

Just then, Mint, Thyme, and Camino emerged through a bright red door at the far end of the room.

"Hi, Camino," I said. "You're looking much better."

"Yes, because the black hen's eggs will work soon," she said. "I'm not too happy that Ruprecht's making me stay here, although I'm grateful to him for his hospitality. I just miss my house."

Ruprecht crossed to her and patted her hand. "Never mind, Camino, you'll be going back home soon enough."

I looked past them to the TV. It was large and modern. At last! I would be able to watch something other than Jamie Oliver.

"Well, what's the plan for tonight, then?" I asked. "If we're all staying here, we might as well make something fun out of it." The others nodded in agreement, but couldn't seem to think of anything. "Well, how about a movie?" I suggested.

"Oh, yes, excellent idea, Amelia!" Ruprecht

responded with delight. "I have a tape of Yasujiro Ozu's *Late Spring* that I've been meaning to watch."

A tape, I thought. I tried not to laugh. It didn't surprise me at all that Ruprecht would still watch movies on tapes, but it made it all the stranger that his TV was the latest technology. I guessed it was also possible that the movie wasn't available digitally or on Blu-ray or something modern.

"I haven't heard of it," Thyme said as she raised an inquisitive eyebrow. "If it's on tape, I assume it isn't new?"

"Oh, no, of course not. It's from 1949." Ruprecht said this as if it were a good thing. "It's a classic, and some consider it to be a criticism of marriage, which of course was topical for Japan in the late 1940's. However, it also comments on tradition versus modernity, which is a subject that anybody can enjoy." His eyes lit up during this entire explanation, though I certainly wasn't convinced that anybody could enjoy these things at all.

"That sounds nice, Ruprecht," I lied, "but do you have any other options?" I tried my best not to sound like I was pleading.

"Well, I also have the *Rush Hour* trilogy."

"Let's watch that," we all said in unison and with great relief.

"Okay, I'll put it on. There are some snacks in the kitchen, just over there to the right." He motioned with his hands to point it out. "Help yourselves, and I'll make tea or coffee if anybody feels like some." He didn't seem at all sad about the prospect of changing films, which was reassuring. As much as I didn't want to watch *Late Spring*, I also didn't want to upset Ruprecht.

We watched the first two movies back-to-back. I'd figured that Jackie Chan movies were always the best way to forget about one's problems, whether said problems were financial, homicidal, romantic, or anything in between. However, they didn't do much to sate hunger, and my stomach started to rumble, despite my earlier intake of cauliflower.

"Oh, dear, look at the time!" Ruprecht suddenly shot out of his seat. "I hadn't realised, but none of you have had dinner. I'll prepare something immediately." He ran—or more accurately, sort of shuffled quickly—out of the room and into the kitchen.

Thyme shot me a look, but I avoided her gaze.

I wasn't about to fess up to the others that I'd had dinner with Alder.

"Do you want help?" I called out to Ruprecht.

"No, no, you're all guests here. Make yourselves comfortable," Ruprecht replied, and I breathed a sigh of relief. I thought it polite to ask, but I didn't want to burn his house down. I realised that perhaps he'd said no because it was me asking, but I just put this at the back of my mind and tried to relax.

We sat and talked about nothing in particular. Nobody wanted to talk about Sue. It was bad enough that Ruprecht believed we might be in danger and had called us here, so maybe it was better that we just tried to relax and forget about it for a night.

I decided to get changed now, before the movie started, and Camino showed me to the bedrooms. She handed me a folded onesie and opened the door to the bathroom. It was surprisingly free of clutter. I had half expected to have to climb a mountain of antiques. To the contrary, it was modern and spacious. I changed into the onesie Camino had lent me. Since it had been folded before, I hadn't realised that it was an echidna onesie, complete with spikes, and a long nose on the hood. I swallowed my pride and put it on, hoping Alder wouldn't happen to stumble through into Ruprecht's house and see me. I knew he wouldn't, but the thought still made me strangely nervous.

I felt a mixture of relief and worry when nobody mentioned how bizarre I looked as an echidna. I figured some of them probably didn't think anything of it, and the others were just too polite. I wasn't even sure why Camino owned something like this, but didn't question the convenience of it.

After another half an hour of painstakingly delicious smells, Ruprecht appeared with several plates. I went into the kitchen and helped him bring out cutlery and drinks. The table in the living room wasn't big enough to seat all of us, but we made space where we could and sat in a rough circle.

"Mediterranean vegetable parcels! I hope you enjoy them." Ruprecht laid a plate down in front of me. Vegetables were packed tightly into a small parcel of rice paper, and coated in herbs. Baby tomatoes, bell peppers, zucchini and more were lightly roasted and topped with herbs and feta cheese. It tasted even better than it smelled, and none of us spoke a word while we ate, though it didn't take long.

"Now, I believe Detectives Lee and Carter were heading to Paris." Ruprecht flicked on the third and final Rush Hour movie, and we watched in silence. Watching Jackie Chan always made me want to learn martial arts, which I thought was probably a good idea. What if I was attacked? After all, I found myself often—far too often— tracking down murderers. I gave up on the idea when I realised baking cakes was too much for me, and that I should focus on improving in one area at a time.

When the movie was over, we sat around and talked for a good while. It seemed obvious that we were all doing our very best to avoid mentioning the murder, or anything related to it.

I said a polite goodnight to everybody, and we were all shown to our rooms. Thyme and I were sharing a guest bedroom, but had separate single beds. We were both too tired to talk and immediately went to bed, but it was a long time before I managed to fall asleep. I had a feeling something bad was about to happen, and I knew it would affect me somehow.

CHAPTER 26

I had spent a strange night in Ruprecht's house. I wondered if his house was somehow related to mine. Not that it did anything, but it reminded me of a Hollywood horror-film house, albeit in a good way. It gave the impression of underground tunnels buried beneath, of ancient priest holes—although there were none of those in Australia—and of hidden secrets possessed by the souls of those who had lived here in days gone by.

It was early morning. I always love this time of day, the quiet before most people are out and about. I got out of my car, yawned, and stretched. I was looking forward to taking a shower and changing my clothes. The onesie I had borrowed from Camino last night was a particularly scratchy one, most likely due to the all too realistic echidna spikes.

I looked at the black clouds gathering in the west. They appeared to be rolling in quickly, and already humidity hung heavily in the air. It was unusual to have humidity in the mountainous region of New South Wales, and I knew a storm was on its way. It was also unusual to have a storm in the morning. The sense of premonition I had felt the previous night was increasing in intensity, and I felt it had nothing to do with the storm.

I stood for a moment to look at my garden. The lavender buds had already wilted, and the rose bushes were starting to get some black spot on their leaves. Nevertheless, many roses were in bloom, and the heartsease, here a winter plant, were still thriving nicely. The bees were happily dancing around the flowers, and a wild duck with about twelve of her ducklings waddled quickly away from me, startled by my sudden appearance.

A strange prescience hit me, but it didn't quite take shape. I walked up my pathway. As soon as I reached my porch, I heard the television blaring loudly. "Give it a rest!" I yelled at the house.

I unlocked the door, and at once noticed that something was wrong. It took me a moment to realise what it was. Where were Willow and Hawthorn? I shrugged. I expected they were giving me the cold shoulder for being absent the previous night.

I went to turn right, off the hallway into my bedroom, but the noise of the television was too much to bear. Instead, I turned left and opened the door to the living room. I walked straight across the room to the TV and turned it off, but even as I did so, I sensed that something was wrong. To my horror, I could smell gasoline. Where were the cats?

I swung around and there, huddled in a corner, was Victor Barnes.

It seemed even stranger to me, in my fright, that Willow and Hawthorn were draped all over him, purring, and he made no attempt to stop them. At first I thought he was dead.

He spoke then, his voice coming out as a faint croaking sound. "Make it stop." It sounded to me as if he had tried to make his tone urgent, but failed. I called the cats away from him, and when they left, I saw his face and hands were covered with a terrible, angry red rash. His face was swollen, and his eyes were streaming. In fact, his eyes had been reduced to slits.

Next to him were a can of gasoline and a box of matches.

He looked to me to be someone who had left his last vestiges of sanity behind.

I stood, frozen to the spot. For a moment I was unsure what to do next. It was clear that the house had terrified Victor in a way that only the house could.

For that reason, I called Ruprecht before I called the police.

"You've done the right thing," Ruprecht said. "In fact, don't call the police until we get there. We'll be right over."

Despite the situation with which I was faced, it didn't seem long before they all arrived. Ruprecht, Mint, Camino, and Thyme burst into the room. In the time it had taken them to get there, Victor had neither moved nor spoken again. His eyes were glazed over.

"Is he dead?" Camino asked me.

"No," I said. "The house has given him a terrible fright, though."

Ruprecht walked over and peered into Victor's face for a while. Finally, he turned to me. "Call the police now, Amelia. Tell them you all had a sleepover at my house, and we all came back here together to find him sitting in the corner of your room next to a can of gasoline and a box of matches. Say as little else as possible."

I did exactly as Ruprecht had asked.

While we were waiting for the police to arrive, Victor just sat there, as he had been, staring into space. "What's going to happen when the police get here?" I asked Ruprecht.

"They will arrest him, of course," he said.

"But why? Won't they call it circumstantial evidence that he has a can of gasoline with him, and what will the police say about him being in that state?"

Ruprecht shook his head. "Let the police draw their own conclusions," he said. "Don't forget that Thyme put the black hen's eggs in Sue's hands, and that means that the murderer will reveal himself. Just wait and trust the process."

I was inclined *not* to trust the process. Even though I was supposed to be a powerful witch, and a Dark Witch at that, I still couldn't for the life of me see that Victor was suddenly going to jump to his feet and blab about his crimes to the police.

Ruprecht seemed to know what I was thinking, because he placed his hand on my shoulder and said, "Just wait and see."

"Should we do something, though?" I asked him. "Should we give him a truth potion or something?"

Camino stepped forward. "No, that won't be necessary. The eggs have done their work already. Just wait."

Her words were drowned by the blare of sirens. Ruprecht went out to meet the police, and soon returned with the two local police officers.

"Is he dead?" Constable Walker asked.

"No," Ruprecht said. "He seems to be having some sort of psychotic episode."

Sergeant Tinsdell and the constable walked over to Victor. His eyes flickered when he saw the two men in uniform bending over him. He finally found his voice. "Make Jamie Oliver stop!" he screamed. He scrambled to his feet and backed against the wall, his hands over his ears. "Make Jamie Oliver stop!" he screamed again, pointing in the direction of the television.

The officers exchanged glances. "Walker, get the psych unit on the phone. Quick!"

Walker nodded and left the room. Sergeant Tinsdell turned to us. "Was he like this when you found him?"

We all nodded. "He could be allergic to cats," I

said. "My two cats were draped all over him." The sergeant looked puzzled, so I added, "You know how cats are always attracted to people who don't like them? And perhaps severe allergies can make someone lose their mind."

The sergeant frowned and turned back to Victor. "Why did you break into Amelia Spelled's house with a gas can?"

Victor finally looked away from the TV and then at the gas can. "She asked my wife, Simone, questions," he said slowly, his eyes darting from side to side. "I thought she must've been in it with Sue Beckett, so I thought I'd get rid of her, too."

The sergeant scratched his chin. "Please go on. What do you mean by saying she was in it with Sue Beckett?"

"The blackmailing racket, of course," he said with a cackle. "At first, Sue Beckett didn't want much money, but she kept asking for more and more. I knew it would never end. I broke into her house and found eleven photos of me, but they were all marked out of twelve, so I knew there was one missing. Anyway, there might've been copies. In the end, I had no choice but to kill her."

"And how did you do that?" the sergeant asked him.

"It was easy." Victor burst into laughter, which became more and more hysterical. We all just stood there looking at him. A chill ran up my spine.

Just as I was beginning to think that he wouldn't say another word, he continued. "Simone keeps Botox in her salon and I just increased the dose. I read that ten times the dose could be dangerous, so I increased it even more than that. After Simone gave Sue the Botox treatment, I destroyed that vial, and replaced it with a standard one."

Constable Walker returned and whispered something in the sergeant's ear.

Sergeant Tinsdell nodded and turned back to Victor. "And why didn't you set fire to Amelia Spelled's house, Victor?"

This appeared to be the wrong thing to say to Victor, as he flung himself back down into his sitting position in the corner once more. "It was the house!" he yelled. "The house wouldn't let me. And then there was Jamie Oliver!"

The officers exchanged glances once more. "Jamie Oliver attacked you?" the sergeant asked him.

"He was so loud. Jamie Oliver was loud. And the house tried to crush me."

The sergeant looked at Constable Walker. "I've heard enough," he said. "He's just babbling utter nonsense now. Let's take him down to the station and wait for the psych people to come and evaluate him."

"I think he's been watching too much TV," Walker said. When Tinsdell quirked an eyebrow, he continued. "You know, thinking he can plead not guilty due to mental illness."

The sergeant shook his head. "No. I think this one really is a burger shy of a combo meal."

The officers led Victor out the door, and all the while Victor was looking around himself muttering wildly about Jamie Oliver being too loud, being allergic to cats, and the house trying to kill him.

CHAPTER 27

We were all sitting around the table in my back yard, shaded by a large blue umbrella slotted into the table. Other than myself, there were four people: Ruprecht, Camino, Thyme, and Mint. We were sitting in the cool of the afternoon, enjoying the breeze. Nobody had spoken for a long time, but it wasn't awkward—simply peaceful.

I had received a text from Alder, which simply stated: *Dinner Friday? No phones, no mysteries.* I smiled again when I thought of it.

We'd had a stressful few weeks, and I think everybody was happy to take a moment just to sit back and relax. Birds were singing happily, and crickets chirped as the wind rustled through the leaves, creating a calm, pleasant atmosphere.

I took a long, slow sip of my coffee and set it gently on the table. *This is what it's all about*, I thought. *Delicious coffee. Oh, and being with my friends.* I looked at everyone and smiled. I'd come a long way from when I'd been evicted from my tiny apartment, and while I still wasn't sure I could handle the cake store, I knew that I'd have the right people supporting me.

"A superior man is modest in his speech, but superior in his actions." Ruprecht broke the silence with another one of his proverbs.

I corrected him. "A superior *person*."

"Quite so," he laughed, "but it still stands true."

I took the bait. "What does it mean, Ruprecht?" I feigned interest, though I honestly enjoyed his philosophical tirades. Sometimes. A little bit. Maybe.

I soon regretted my question.

"Well, it's fairly straightforward." He put his coffee down, straightened his back, and cleared his throat. I sighed softly and prepared myself for the incoming monologue. "The superior man—excuse me, person—is the one who can prove themselves through actions without relying on words. This isn't to say that words can't be used to great effect, or necessarily that actions speak louder than words, but that the superior person can prove themselves through their actions *rather* than just their words. Now, there's a slightly more complicated deeper meaning here..."

He continued for what felt like hours, but was probably only about ten minutes. I occasionally caught myself letting my mind wander and would try to refocus, but everything he was saying had become a kind of mush of uninteresting philosophical musings. At one point, I even considered asking for Thyme's advice on baking just to change the subject, but I realised that would probably excite her to the same level as Ruprecht, and nothing would change, except perhaps my property value after I tried to bake again.

"And how does that relate to our situation?" Camino asked earnestly. I think she'd been listening the entire time, but it was possible she had mastered the art of pretending. Maybe her hearing was starting to go, which I now realised could sometimes be a blessing.

"Oh, well to be honest, I thought that would be fairly obvious, but I'm glad you asked." Ruprecht took another sip of coffee before he continued. "I was thinking about Victor."

"You think Victor is a superior man?" I asked, eyebrows raised.

"Oh, no, quite the opposite. I was thinking about not only Victor, but also about you, Amelia. Victor was less than a nice person, to put it lightly, as I'm sure we all agree. However, I'm also sure we'd all agree that you're a wonderful person."

I shifted uncomfortably. I was never very good at taking compliments.

"You're obviously two very different people," he continued. "But this quote, which is from Confucius, believe it or not,"—*I can believe it*, I thought—"pertains to our situation. Victor is a coward, and attempted to do something incomprehensibly horrible both to you and your property."

"And to my cats," I interjected.

"Of course, and to your cats. Luckily, or rather, by some other force, he was thwarted. That makes the third criminal you've helped to apprehend, and yet I never hear you brag about it." Ruprecht smiled at me proudly.

"Well, I didn't realise I was allowed to brag. Now that I know, I'll make a point of doing so," I joked. It meant a lot to hear Ruprecht praise me, even if he was doing it in his own roundabout way. "Now, would anybody like another coffee? There's plenty left in the kitchen, which is right next to the room in which I apprehended a criminal mastermind."

Everybody laughed. "I wouldn't call him a mastermind," Thyme said, still laughing. "His evil master plan was thwarted by a house and two cats."

"No, not just the cats and the house. Also Jamie Oliver," I added.

As much as we were making light of the situation, it was a little unsettling that there had been so much violence in the short amount of time since I'd moved here. If this kept up, I wasn't sure I'd want to stay, though I would probably make a better detective than a baker. I'm not certain which made more money, but I know which I'd rather do, and it's the one with fewer people dying.

"What's bothering you, Amelia?" Mint asked kindly.

"It's just all of this crime lately. Since I've moved here, we've had more murders than most people experience in their lifetime. Tell me this isn't normal for this town."

"No, it isn't," she replied. "It's been very troubled here lately, but I don't think you have anything to worry about. Certainly not in your own house!" She smiled as she said it, and she was right. Nobody had any reason to hurt me, but even if someone tried, I was safe in my house. More than that though, I always had my friends beside me.

NEXT BOOK IN THIS SERIES

THE KITCHEN WITCH BOOK 4

Spelling Mistake

Amelia Spelled discovers an old spellbook, which to her delight contains a spell to improve one's baking. When a spelling mistake is thrown into the mix, she accidentally summons an entity. Amelia does her best to reverse the spell, but finds it's no piece of cake. When a murderer strikes, can Amelia rise to the occasion, solve the murder, and find her abilities as a witch?

ABOUT MORGANA BEST

USA Today Bestselling author Morgana Best survived a childhood of deadly spiders and venomous snakes in the Australian outback.

Morgana Best writes cozy mysteries and enjoys thinking of delightful new ways to murder her victims.

www.morganabest.com

Made in the USA
Las Vegas, NV
11 August 2021

27968624R00146